SUZANNE ROSS JONES

SEE YOU IN MY DREAMS

D0526747

Complete and Unabridged

LINFORD
Leicester

First published in Great Britain in 2014

First Linford Edition
published 2015

A catalogue record for this book is available
from the British Library.

ISBN 978–1–4448–2405–6

Published by
F. A. Thorpe (Publishing)
Anstey, Leicestershire

Set by Words & Graphics Ltd.
Anstey, Leicestershire
Printed and bound in Great Britain by
T. J. International Ltd., Padstow, Cornwall

This book is printed on acid-free paper

SEE YOU IN MY DREAMS

When Vicky Simpson arrives from Edinburgh as a worried relative in nurse Ryan McGregor's hospital, there's an immediate attraction between the two. As a trained nurse herself, Vicky stays to help care for her brother-in-law. It proves impossible for Vicky and Ryan to avoid each other, and their attraction. But Vicky doesn't intend to stay in Aberbrig, and Ryan is firmly settled there. Should they nurture their growing romance? Or should they end things before someone gets hurt?

1

A Nurse's Life

There was no such thing as a slow start for a nurse at the beginning of a shift. But, as soon as he stepped into A&E, Ryan McGregor knew today was going to be extra busy.

'We've had a standby call from the paramedics,' Faye, his fellow staff nurse and housemate told him as she hurried by. 'They're bringing in a thirty-year-old male; the victim of a fall. He's unconscious, with possible head, neck and back injuries. They should be here in five to ten minutes.'

Ryan swung into action and headed to the resuscitation room to prepare for the imminent arrival. He made sure all the equipment and supplies they might need were ready, then he went out to the ambulance doors.

There was an autumnal chill in the air; it seeped through the thin material of his scrubs and made the hairs stand up on his bare arms. He stamped his feet to keep his circulation going.

They should be here any minute.

Ryan worked in emergency medicine because he loved it. He loved how busy they were. He loved the variety of dealing with all sorts of patients and the challenge of thinking on his feet. And he loved that every shift was different.

But he definitely didn't love the wait to see how badly someone might be injured.

When the ambulance arrived, Ryan hopped on board to help. And he stopped dead when he saw who it was.

'Steven Craig,' he said, before pulling himself together and getting on with the job in hand.

'He's a roofer,' one of the paramedics filled in, though Ryan knew that already. 'Fell a good twenty feet onto his right side and he's hit his head in the process. He's been slipping in and out of consciousness.'

Steven was strapped to a spinal board, his neck in a collar and his head taped to head blocks — this would immobilise him and limit the chance of any further damage as they moved him.

'Steven,' Ryan said, and the man's eyes fluttered. 'It's Ryan. You're at the hospital. We're going to take you inside now.'

Steven groaned incoherently.

'Hurts,' he mumbled.

'Don't worry, we're going to take good care of you.' Ryan was careful not to tell the patient that he'd be fine — he never made promises he couldn't keep. And, until he was assessed properly, nobody could know what the full extent of Steven's injuries might be.

'Claire,' Steven muttered.

'Don't worry, someone will call her,' Ryan said. 'Claire's his wife,' he supplied, for the benefit of the paramedics. 'She works for my brother.'

Once they got the patient into the resuscitation room, everyone fell into their roles. Ryan started to cut Steven's clothing, then the nurses and the paramedics worked together to roll the patient over so the doctor could carefully examine his spine.

'We'll have to wait for the x-rays before we can remove the collar,' the doctor said.

'Hurts really badly,' Steven groaned loudly.

The doctor gave instructions for painkillers to be given and then the preliminary x-rays were taken.

'They're not conclusive,' the doctor gave her verdict to the team. 'We'll have to take him to radiology.'

Faye went down with him while Ryan went to see if Claire had arrived.

He found her in the waiting room — pale and trembling and pacing the floor. She was too preoccupied to even notice that Ryan was there.

'Where is everyone?' she said. 'Why don't they tell us how he is?'

Ryan was pleased to see she wasn't alone — Paula, Ryan's soon-to-be sister-in-law, was speaking to her in a soothing voice.

'He's in the best place,' Paula said calmly. 'I'm sure they'll let us know as soon as there's any news.' At that moment, Paula noticed Ryan and got to her feet.

Taking her cue from her friend, Claire spun around.

'Ryan,' she said as she flew across to him. Then she stood for a moment and took a deep breath, before speaking: 'How's Steven?'

★   ★   ★

Vicky was busy with a paintbrush when the call came. She was keen to get her bedroom all cosy and decorated before winter set in.

It was probably the agency with a job for her, she decided.

She rested the brush carefully on the top of the tin of paint and dug her phone from the back pocket of her jeans. She glanced at the display and saw it wasn't the agency after all. It was her sister, Claire.

Vicky frowned. Claire never called during the day.

'What's up?' she said. There was a sob from the other end. Her heart filled with dread. 'Claire,' she said, 'what's wrong?'

There was another sob as Claire tried to speak, but Vicky couldn't make out a single word.

'Claire,' she said again, panic making her sound sharp, 'tell me what's wrong.'

'Steven,' Claire managed between sniffs. 'He's been in an accident and he's really hurt. Vicky, I'm scared he's not going to make it.'

This was the one single reason Vicky wasn't happy she lived so far away from her sister; when there was a family emergency, she couldn't just pop round in five minutes. But she knew she had to go — there was nobody else.

Her mind was helplessly drawn back to the last time family members had been involved in an accident. She and

Claire had lost both their parents that time. So it was understandable that her sister would fear the worst now.

'Claire,' she said, trying to keep her voice calm, 'hold on, sweetie. I'll be with you as soon as I can.'

The only time she'd been back to Aberbrig in the past seven years had been for Claire's wedding. And that time it had been a flying visit — she'd left as soon as the happy couple had departed on their honeymoon. This time, though, she might need to stay a few days.

She hurriedly wrote a note for her flatmates, then threw a few things into an overnight bag: a couple of changes of clothes, her toothbrush and toiletries. Then she phoned the agency to let them know she wouldn't be available until further notice.

It was only when she was out of Edinburgh and on the road north that she realised she hadn't even changed out of her paint-splattered jeans and t-shirt.

She arrived at Aberbrig General Hospital a few hours later, weary and nearly frantic with concern for her brother-in-law and worry about how her sister was coping.

Of course, the car park was full. She groaned in frustration as she drove around trying to find a space. Just when she was on the verge of giving up, a small red car pulled out and drove off. With a sigh of relief, she drove her little blue Mini in and hurried towards the building.

As soon as she flew through the door, she bumped into someone. A tall someone with a shock of dark red hair and blue eyes that looked down at her with a slightly disapproving air.

Ryan McGregor hadn't changed a bit. And he was still able to make her feel horribly self-conscious with only a glance in her direction. Particularly as she was aware she'd left home in such a rush that she was a complete mess.

Which was all ridiculous: she was a confident, independent woman. More to the point, she was here for her sister. So why should she care what Ryan McGregor thought?

'Steady on, there,' he said as he reached out to help her regain her balance.

'I'm sorry,' she mumbled, while mentally telling herself sternly to get over her embarrassment.

Besides, if he recognised her, he wasn't showing any sign of it.

'I wonder if you can help,' she said. 'I'm looking for my sister, Claire Craig. Her husband, Steven, has been in an accident.'

He gave a short nod.

'She's in the waiting room,' he told her. Still not showing any sign that he knew her. But then why should he? He'd barely known she existed when they'd been at school so it wasn't likely he'd remember her now so many years later. 'Come on, I'll show you.'

Vicky struggled to keep up as he covered the distance in several long strides. But she forgot all thoughts of

Ryan as she saw her sister — her cool, calm and normally unflappable sister — in a nervous heap in the corner of the room.

Another woman sat with her as Claire trembled uncontrollably. But then a fleeting look of hope crossed her face as she spotted Ryan McGregor making his way towards her.

'The doctor's still with Steven,' he said. 'But I've someone here to see you.'

And that was when Claire looked away from Ryan long enough to see he wasn't alone.

'You're here.' Claire was on her feet, her face alarmingly pale — apart from the red nose of someone who had been crying for hours.

Vicky held out her arms and Claire collapsed into them, with a renewed bout of sobbing.

'Thank you so much for coming,' she said as she lifted her head and sniffed.

Vicky held onto her sister with one arm and searched in her pocket for a clean tissue with her free hand.

'Don't be silly,' Vicky said gently. 'How could I not come?' Emerging from her search triumphant, she handed the tissue over and Claire quickly mopped her face.

There was no doubting Vicky owed her sister big time. She'd been fifteen when they'd lost their parents. Claire had only been three years older, but she'd left school, found a job and had convinced the authorities she was able to look after Vicky. And she'd done a marvellous job.

'I'll leave you to it,' Ryan said quietly. 'I'll be back in as soon as there's any news.'

Vicky looked up at him while she continued to hug the distressed Claire.

'Thank you,' she said. And he inclined his head in acknowledgement before he left.

She guided her sister back to her chair and made her sit down.

'Can I get you something? Some water? A coffee?'

'No, thank you.' Claire shook her

head. 'Paula's been looking after me. I'm fine.' She looked anything but fine as she glanced from Vicky to the other woman. 'I'm sorry, I should have introduced you. This is Paula — Jack McGregor's fiancée,' she mentioned her boss and Ryan's brother. 'Paula, this is my sister, Vicky.'

Introductions made, Vicky sat down.

'So, how is he?' she asked. 'And what happened?'

* ★ *

Ryan wasn't surprised that Vicky Simpson hadn't recognised him; he'd been in the year above her at school and they'd barely spoken. But he'd noticed her; it had been impossible not to — she'd always been a pretty girl.

But she'd been as prickly as a hedgehog. Any boy who'd asked her out had been given short shrift as she'd been determined to keep up with her studies, intent on conquering the world.

And then her parents had died and

her whole world had changed.

The last he'd heard, she'd gone to Edinburgh to start training as a nurse. And she hadn't been in any hurry to come back over the years. But it wasn't surprising she was here now; even if she wasn't fond of Aberbrig, she'd always loved her sister.

'It seems things aren't as bad with your friend, Steven, as they might have been,' Faye told him as he looked in. 'The orthopaedic consultant's been to see him. The right humerus and femur have fractures and his elbow and knee have compound fractures. Theatre's all booked up today, so he'll need to wait until tomorrow to have the compound fractures pinned into a better position.'

This was good news. With such a fall, Steven's injuries could have been so much worse.

'I'll go and tell his wife,' he said.

Claire, Paula and Vicky were still pretty much where he'd left them.

'We'll need to keep Steven in for a while. But he's young and strong and there's no reason he won't make a full recovery in time.'

He was shocked when Claire flew at him and hugged him tight, knocking the wind out of him in the process.

'Thank you, Ryan,' she said. 'Thank you so much. I'll never forget what you've done today.'

'Thanks,' he said, feeling embarrassed that he was being singled out for praise. 'But it was a team effort.'

2

A Nice Cup of Tea

Working at the hospital stressed the fragility of life and the importance of family to Ryan on a daily basis. That was why, instead of heading home after his shift, he drove the few miles to Kinbrae.

Rather than driving through the main street and out towards the McGregor family farmhouse, he brought the car to a stop outside the café. It had been in his family for generations until Paula had bought it a few months ago, but it still bore the McGregor name over the door.

This was very apt as she would be joining the family when she married his older brother, Jack, in a few months.

He knew Paula was still with Claire, so his mother must working at the café today. He'd have his evening meal here with her, rather than back at his place where he'd end up talking shop — or hospital — with the other nurses he shared with.

'Hello sweetheart,' Heather McGregor said as he walked through the door. 'I wasn't expecting to see you.'

'It's been a busy day. I needed some space.'

'What can I get you? Cup of tea?'

'Thanks, Ma.' He grinned. There were no customers this late in the day and he sat at a table near the window. 'And a bacon roll, please.'

'I'll put an egg in it, too,' she said with a smile and ruffled his hair as she walked past.

He laughed softly as she made her way through to the kitchen. As the youngest of Heather's three sons, Ryan often suspected his mother still thought of him as a child, rather than as a grown man of twenty-five. The ruffling of his hair would seem to bear that suspicion out.

As his mother disappeared through the door, Paula came in from outside, bringing in the cold air of the late autumn afternoon with her. She stopped when she saw Ryan sitting there.

'Hello,' she said, pulling out a chair and sitting down at the same table. 'Didn't think I'd see you again so soon.'

'Just felt like dropping by to see Mum,' he said. 'Some days get you like that.'

Paula reached out and patted his arm.

'It was a rough day all round.'

'How's Claire doing now?'

'Vicky's taken her home.' Paula sighed. 'Though I doubt either of them will get any rest tonight.'

'Steven will be OK.'

'I know that.' Paula nodded. 'But Claire's finding it difficult to believe.'

'It's always a shock when a loved one needs hospital treatment. Lucky you were with her when she got the call to

17

say he was injured.'

Paula smiled.

'We were looking at bridesmaids' dresses,' Paula revealed. 'Just getting an idea of what's out there before we go on a proper shopping trip with the other girls.' She sighed. 'Though I don't know now if Claire will even be able to come to the wedding — let alone be my maid of honour.'

'The wedding's not for months,' Ryan reminded her. 'Steven will be well on the mend by then. Though he might have to go to the service in a wheelchair.'

Heather came out of the kitchen bearing a tray with teapot, cup and saucer, and Ryan's bacon and egg roll.

'Hi, Paula,' she said. 'How did you and Claire get on with your shopping trip?'

Paula looked across at Ryan uncertainly.

'I haven't said anything to Mum about Steven,' he told her.

Heather's eyes narrowed.

'What's going on?'

Quickly, Paula filled her future mother-in-law in on what had happened as Heather poured tea for Ryan.

'Oh, that's dreadful,' she said, sitting down at one of the two spare chairs left at the table.

'Could have been worse.' Ryan was philosophical. Though he shuddered as he tried not to think exactly how much worse it could have been.

'Luckily Claire's sister managed to get there fairly quickly, considering how far she had to travel,' Paula added, going over to fetch cups for herself and Heather.

'Vicky?' Heather asked.

'Yes,' Paula confirmed. 'Do you know her?'

'No, but I've heard Claire speak of her. She's a nurse, too.' Heather glanced across at Ryan.

He nodded to confirm what his mother had said.

'She's a pretty little thing,' Paula said.

Yes, Ryan reflected on his brief meeting with Claire's sister as he bit into his roll, Vicky was extraordinarily pretty — even more so now than she'd been at school. Not that he was in the habit of noticing the pretty relatives of patients; that sort of behaviour wasn't in the least professional. So it only went to show just how attractive Claire's sister was.

The bell rang, heralding the arrival of another customer. All three looked up to see Josh Carter, the village GP.

'Good afternoon, Doctor,' Heather said as she went to get up, but Paula beat her to it.

'Sit,' she told Heather.

'But . . . ' Heather looked a little startled and Ryan suppressed a grin. It was a change to see his mother lost for words — or giving in to orders to take things easy.

'You've been on your feet since first thing this morning,' Paula said a little more softly. 'It's my turn to serve now.' She turned to her customer and smiled.

'Now, Doctor, what can I get for you?'

As Paula busied herself with getting tea and a fruit scone for the doctor, Heather disregarded orders and began to tidy the café.

'I'm glad I've seen you,' Josh Carter said to Ryan. 'I'm going to be short of a nurse at the surgery soon. Elise handed her notice in — her husband's being transferred.'

Ryan could see where this was heading. Before Elise's arrival, the doctor had suggested Ryan apply for the post. Part of him had been tempted by the thought of the regular hours of a practice nurse, but he'd known immediately that would not be the right move for him. His heart lay in the A&E department.

'I'm sure you'll find someone suitable to replace her,' he said with a smile.

'Don't suppose you're fed up of working at the hospital yet?'

'Afraid not.' He grinned.

'Pity.' The doctor shook his head. 'Well, no harm in asking. I suppose

21

we'll have to go through an agency and hope they have someone suitable. We need to find someone quickly. Elise wants to leave as soon as she can.'

* * *

As soon as they got back to Claire's house, Vicky put the kettle on.

How odd it all was; when she'd woken this morning, her thoughts had been filled with her plans to decorate her room. It hadn't even occurred to her that she'd be ending the day in her sister's home.

She glanced across at Claire, who was still pale and trembling.

'They would tell you, you know.'

Claire looked up, a puzzled frown on her face.

'Who would tell me what?' She reached out and took the mug of hot tea that Vicky held out to her.

'The staff at the hospital would tell you the truth if there was something you needed to be worried about.'

'He's my husband, Vicky, and he's hurt. Of course I need to be worried. And you know how it ended the last time we had to visit someone in hospital after they'd been in an accident.'

Vicky went over to her sister and gave her a quick hug.

'He needs time, but he will be OK. Broken bones will mend and he'll be good as new.'

Claire sniffed loudly and covered the hand Vicky had put on her shoulder with her own.

'Thank you for coming when I phoned. I was worried about asking. I know how hard it is for you to come back. But I'm so glad you're here.'

Vicky felt terrible that her sister might have even doubted for a second that she'd come. She resolved that, once this was all over, somehow or other she and Vicky would have to see more of each other. It was important for sisters to be close even if they lived so many miles apart.

'I'm glad I'm here, too,' she said. 'Now, let me run you a nice hot bath and, while you're soaking, I'll make us some supper.'

'I can run my own bath,' Claire said.

'You need to take care of yourself and you need to let me spoil you a bit,' Vicky told her. 'Once Steven's home, he's going to need a lot of help and it's going to be tough on you.'

Claire nodded.

'I know,' she said. 'And I just can't wait.'

⋆ ⋆ ⋆

Two of the nurses Ryan shared the house with were at work when he arrived home, but he found Faye in the kitchen.

'I've brought plum cake back from the café for us to have with our coffee,' he told her.

'A Heather McGregor special?' Faye asked cautiously, obviously containing her excitement until she knew the full facts.

Ryan laughed.

'What else?' He could understand Faye's response — everyone knew his mother was the best cake maker within a hundred-mile radius of Kinbrae. Even the bakers here in Aberbrig paled by comparison. So it was understandable Faye would want to know the authenticity of the cake's origin before reacting with too much enthusiasm.

'Great!' Faye grinned. 'I haven't tried her plum cake before.'

'Her garden's full of ripe fruit just now, so she's using them up as quickly as she can.' He'd spotted the cake in Paula's display just as he was leaving the café. His mother had baked it that very afternoon, apparently.

'Suddenly I'm looking forward to my coffee more than ever.' Faye smiled.

'I'll put the kettle on,' Ryan said.

'Do you fancy going out tonight?' Faye asked as she tucked into her unexpected snack, obviously not bothered about waiting for her coffee.

'I don't know. Today's been tough. I was planning an early night.'

'It's always rough when you know a patient personally,' Faye sympathised. 'That's why we could both do with some cheering up.'

He nodded.

'OK. But let's not make it a late one; we do both need to work tomorrow.'

He was lucky to have a friend like Faye — someone who understood the stresses of the job.

They went to a quiet bar around the corner and ordered drinks. Ryan was glad Faye had suggested this; it was good to be out even if only briefly.

He stifled a yawn as he looked around the place. He only wished he wasn't too tired to enjoy it.

'Did you hear anything about how Claire's doing?' Faye asked.

'Yes, I saw Paula when I popped over to Kinbrae after work and she said Vicky was doing a great job looking after her.'

Faye nodded.

Claire and Steven's house wasn't too far from here and it did occur to him that it might be a good idea to pop round to see how the sisters were doing. But then he decided they would probably prefer to be left alone for tonight.

Besides, he didn't really know them well enough to intrude in that way. And no doubt Jack and Paula would be checking up on Claire in the morning, so he could ask his brother for any news.

'It's good that Vicky was able to come to Aberbrig to be with Claire. It must be nice to have family on the same continent to call on.' Faye gave a huge sigh.

Ryan smiled sympathetically.

'Your parents and brothers might be the other side of the world, but you know your friends are here for you whenever you need us.'

She nodded.

'Thanks,' she said. 'That means a lot.'

They didn't stay long. Both were exhausted after their long day and wanted to get home for a proper night's sleep so that they would be ready for tomorrow's shift. They left the bar and walked a little way along the high street.

The mini supermarket was still open and that reminded Ryan he needed to get some shopping.

'We need orange juice,' he said. 'I finished the carton with breakfast this morning. And we could do with bread and milk, too.'

He was surprised when the first person he saw inside the shop was Vicky, paying at the checkout.

She'd changed out of her earlier paint-splattered outfit into a clean pair of jeans and a jumper, but her pale blonde hair was still tied up in its untidy pony tail. He found the whole look unbearably endearing and he had to suppress the sudden urge to give her a spontaneous hug. He settled for a friendly smile instead.

'Hello,' he said as he and Faye

approached. 'How's Claire doing?'

She glanced up at him, a puzzled frown on her face. Just because he remembered her was no guarantee that she would remember him from earlier.

'I'm Ryan,' he said. 'And this is Faye. We work at the hospital and we were there when Steven was brought in.'

'Yes, I know who you are.' She gave a brief nod. 'I just wasn't expecting to see you here.'

'Is everything OK?' Faye asked gently.

'Claire needs chocolate,' she said. 'There was none in the house, so she sent me shopping.'

On some level that made sense to Ryan. It was probably the same instinct that had sent him back to Kinbrae for fast food Heather McGregor style. Comfort eating helped a lot when you were having a tough day.

* * *

Vicky smiled.

'If you'll excuse me,' she said as she

picked up her shopping bag. 'I should be getting back or Claire will wonder where I've got to.'

Even though she was tired and it had been a horrible day, she spent the short walk back to Claire's house trying not to laugh. Fancy Ryan McGregor thinking he had to introduce himself — thinking she might have forgotten him.

And he had a girlfriend. The urge to laugh dissipated. Not that she was surprised he was seeing someone — when he'd been at school he'd been one of the popular boys, and girls had flocked around him.

Not Vicky herself, of course. She'd liked the look of him very much — but from afar. She would never have made an idiot of herself by hanging around him. Especially when she knew her feelings wouldn't have been reciprocated in a million years.

The nurse he was seeing was nice. She'd been very kind today at the hospital. Vicky was glad because he deserved to be happy.

Giving herself a mental shake, she put her head down as she hurried back along the main street to Claire's. It was none of her business.

Despite her supposed need for chocolate, Claire was fast asleep by the time Vicky arrived back. There seemed little point in disturbing her. The sofa was big enough and Vicky worried that if she woke her sister now, Claire might not get back to sleep tonight.

She picked a fleecy throw from the back of a chair and tucked it in around Claire before she turned off the television and the lamps. Then she tiptoed from the room and headed upstairs to the cosy bed that waited for her in her sister's spare room.

3

Aberbrig

Aberbrig had changed a great deal in the years Vicky had been away. As they'd made their way back from the hospital yesterday, she'd hardly dared to believe the changes in the place.

There was the new shopping centre for starters — it was too shiny and new to be true. But the seaside town had retained its character, too, with tiny independent shops and restaurants along the front overlooking the water.

It wasn't a bad place at all, she realised. If only there weren't so many sad memories attached to it. Being here again brought back thoughts of difficult teenage years. But mainly, being back here reminded her too much of the parents she and Claire had lost.

'Do you think you might move back

here?' Claire asked over breakfast the next morning.

Vicky shrugged.

Even though they were sisters with similar upbringings, they had dealt with their grief in very different ways. Claire had held on tight to the familiar, while Vicky had needed distance.

'I really don't know,' she said. 'I can't see it if I'm brutally honest. But it would be nice to live closer to you.'

Claire stirred her coffee for what seemed like the hundredth time.

'You're happy in Edinburgh?'

'I am, for the time being, at least,' Vicky said with a smile. 'I really like my friends and my home. And Edinburgh's a fantastic city. But as you know, I'm looking for a new job and, if I find something interesting, I might go where the work is.'

There was a brief silence and she cast a worried eye towards Claire. Her sister looked pale and weary — as well she might. And she hadn't eaten a single thing this morning.

'Try to eat a bit of toast,' Vicky urged.

'I'm not hungry.'

'Maybe not, but you'll make yourself ill if you don't eat anything.'

'My husband's going to theatre today,' Claire reminded her. 'I really don't feel like eating.'

'Just take a bite,' Vicky coaxed.

Claire sighed, then bit into her toast and chewed mechanically. Then she signalled her meal was at an end by pushing her plate away.

'Do you know, I've been thinking, Vic,' she said. 'You need to find a man. A Aberbrig man. Someone who will make you want to stay.'

Vicky laughed.

In truth, an Aberbrig man was the last kind she'd settle with. Though she hadn't quite given up on the idea of meeting someone special.

She was inspired by the relationship her sister shared with Steven. Even after all these years, it was clear they were still in love. When they had briefly been allowed to visit him once he was taken up to the ward, Vicky's breath had caught as she'd seen the tenderness in his eyes as he'd looked at Claire.

That was what she hoped for one day for herself — a husband who loved her and who she would love in return. Someone tall and handsome and kind. Someone very much like Ryan McGregor.

And then she stopped herself thinking that way, appalled. She'd only last night bumped into him while he'd been on a night out with his girlfriend, for goodness' sake. Thinking of him in that way wasn't appropriate in the least.

'No chance.' She grinned at Claire. 'I'm not disrupting my life for any man.'

'That's what I said once,' Claire said. 'But then I met and married Steven. And look at me now. A complete wreck because my husband's in hospital about to undergo surgery to have his shattered bones pinned.'

'You're not a wreck. You've had a

nasty shock. Once your subconscious realises that Steven is going to be OK, then you'll able to get back to normal.'

Claire sighed. 'I'd better phone Jack and let him know I won't be at work for a few days.'

'Won't his fiancee or his brother have told him about the accident?'

'Maybe. But I should still speak to him.' She still didn't move, though. 'What about Ryan?' she asked at last.

Vicky wrinkled her nose.

'What about him?'

'You used to like him when you were at school.'

She didn't know where that had come from. She'd never even mentioned Ryan — or the fact she'd admired him from afar — to her sister.

'What makes you say that?' she asked, trying to stop her face from flushing a deep red.

'I just thought you had a soft spot for him.' Claire looked a little confused. 'Well, if you fell for him you'd have to stay in the area. Mark's not around much,' she said, naming the middle McGregor brother. 'But Jack and Ryan would never move away. They're both too settled and too fond of their jobs.'

'I told you, I wouldn't stay for a man.' Vicky shook her head. 'And you got it right — I *used* to like the look of him. When I was fourteen or fifteen. Though he didn't notice I existed.' But, even though she knew that was all true, she still remembered how strong his hands had been when he'd reached out to steady her yesterday. And how kind he'd been. Then she added her final argument, more to convince herself rather than Claire: 'And, even if I was tempted, he has a girlfriend.'

Claire seemed puzzled.

'I don't think so. Jack hasn't mentioned he's seeing anyone.'

'Maybe Jack doesn't know. Or maybe he's decided not to gossip about his family to his employees.'

That brought a welcome smile to her sister's face.

'You're forgetting that I can get information from a stone,' she said. 'Let alone my boss.'

Vicky smiled back, pleased her sister's mood had lifted a little.

'So,' Claire continued, 'how long are you staying?'

'As long as you need me,' she replied without hesitation.

She might not be prepared to change her life for any man, but if her sister needed her, she would stay. There was no question of doing anything else. Just as Claire hadn't hesitated to take on a fifteen-year-old when they'd lost their parents — despite the fact she'd still been a teenager herself.

With a sigh, Claire picked up her mobile and called her boss.

'Jack was lovely about it,' she revealed as she hung up. 'He said I was to take as much time as I needed.' The relieved tone was obvious. 'And when Steven's discharged, he's happy for me to work part-time from home for as long as I need.'

'He sounds like a nice boss,' Vicky said.

'He is. The McGregors are a lovely family.'

★　★　★

It had been a long day. Steven was still groggy from the anaesthetic, but Claire was sitting by his bedside, holding his uninjured hand. Vicky had felt she was intruding on a private moment, so had made for the hospital's dining room.

'Tea, please,' she asked, scrambling in her handbag for her purse. It didn't seem to be there. Then she remembered she'd taken it out to dash to the shop last night. It was probably still on the kitchen counter, next to the chocolate she'd bought for her sister.

'Let me get that for you.'

She turned to find Ryan McGregor behind her in the queue. It was on the tip of her tongue to refuse; she was embarrassed about accepting help from him. But the prospect of a tea-less wait ahead changed her mind.

'Thank you, that's kind of you. I seem to have forgotten my purse.'

He smiled and she found herself smiling back. It was hard not to — his grin was infectious.

'Would you mind if I joined you? Breaks can get a bit boring if you have to sit on your own.'

She would have preferred not to sit with him, but how could she say no when he'd paid for her tea?

He carried a tray laden with two teas over to a corner table and she followed, sitting opposite him.

'How's your sister today?'

'A bit better than when I arrived yesterday. She knows Steven's out of immediate danger now, so she's been able to relax a bit.'

He nodded.

'And how are you doing?'

She was touched that he was showing concern for her.

'I'm fine.' She smiled. 'Worried about

Claire and Steven, obviously. But I'm very glad that if something like this had to happen, at least I'm in a position to stay with Claire for as long as she needs me. That's one massive positive to not having a permanent job.'

Ryan raised an eyebrow.

'I worked as a practice nurse,' she told him. 'But it was a large GP practice and I found I was landed with the same jobs day after day.'

Ryan nodded.

'I can see that would become monotonous.'

'Don't get me wrong,' she added hastily. 'I loved dealing with people and helping them. It was just, as a clinician, I wanted more variety and more experience.'

'Where are you working now?'

'In Edinburgh, for an agency. But I'm looking for something permanent.' Giving in her notice at the surgery without having found another job probably hadn't been the wisest move she'd ever made. But agency nursing

41

had worked out well for her in the short term.

Long term, though, she knew she needed to get her teeth into a fulfilling job; something that would challenge her and somewhere she could carve a niche and feel she would be challenged.

Ryan was looking at her with a thoughtful expression and it worried her.

'What?' she asked.

But he didn't answer straight away. Instead, he sat back in his chair and drummed on the table top for a few seconds.

*   *   *

Ryan was reluctant to tell Vicky about the job Josh Carter had talked to him about. He didn't know why: if she wasn't interested she didn't have to apply.

'I might know of a job,' he said at last. 'In this area — not Edinburgh.'

'At the hospital?'

He shook his head.

'At the surgery in Kinbrae. It would be regular hours — and it would mean that you would be back in the area, near your sister.'

She didn't look too happy at the prospect. His gut instinct had been right — he shouldn't have said anything.

'I don't know . . . I hadn't thought of looking for work around here.'

'No problem,' he said. 'I only thought I'd mention it when you said you were looking. Josh, the GP, only spoke to me about it yesterday, so I know he won't have found anyone else, and I thought you might be interested.'

She was thoughtful for a moment.

'I might be,' she said. 'It seems daft not to find out more. And even if I applied there would be no guarantee I'd get it in any case.'

Ryan could recognise someone trying to talk themselves around and he didn't say anything, letting her say what she needed to say.

'Claire would be happy if I got a job around here. And maybe they would consider taking me on a temporary basis.'

'I know Josh needs to find a nurse quickly, so he may well be happy to consider a temporary contract.'

He glanced at his watch. His break was nearly over.

'Can you meet for a quick drink when I've finished work?' he asked. 'Then I can give you the details.'

She started to nod, then she brushed back her pale blonde hair and looked up at him with troubled blue eyes.

'Won't your girlfriend mind if we meet for a drink?' She looked shocked she'd asked the question — as shocked as he felt.

'What girlfriend?'

'The nurse you were out with last night. Faye.'

He smiled and she looked confused.

'Faye's not my girlfriend,' he said. 'She's my friend. And one of the crowd I share a house with.'

Vicky Simpson was even more stunning when she smiled.

'OK, Ryan,' she said almost shyly. 'Thank you. That would be very helpful.'

* * *

Vicky felt rather foolish as she made her way back to the ward where Steven was being looked after. She should have listened to Claire about Ryan not having a girlfriend.

And then she felt foolish for quite a different reason. Even if he'd had a girlfriend, he hadn't been asking her out on a date. He was being friendly and trying to help a fellow nurse find work.

Her face burned. Because the reason for her concern was pretty obvious once she thought about it. Had she not found him attractive, she wouldn't have thought twice about Faye maybe being his girlfriend. But because she'd always liked the look of him, it had been at the forefront of her mind.

She didn't want to tell Claire about her meeting — neither the one at the canteen, nor the one planned for early evening. She imagined, after their conversation earlier, that her sister would jump to all sorts of conclusions.

But there was no reasonable way she could go out for an hour or two without explaining things. It wasn't like she could be vague about it, either, though she tried. Because Claire had been right — she could get information out of a stone.

'What do you mean you're going to see a friend?' Claire's eyes narrowed suspiciously. 'What friend, exactly?'

'Just a friend.' She refused to engage with Claire's inquisitive gaze and continued to apply mascara, using her tiny handbag mirror.

'But you haven't kept in touch with anyone. Steven and I are the only people you know here these days.'

That much was true. Vicky's final years in Aberbrig had been so miserable as she'd grieved that she hadn't wanted any reminder of the place. Not even a card or letter from the crew she'd occasionally hung around with.

'And you haven't been anywhere to bump into anyone. Unless . . . '

She could almost hear the wheels of her sister's mind working as she put two and two together and made a hundred and five.

'It's Ryan, isn't it?' she demanded.

Vicky glanced over.

'Maybe.'

Claire laughed. And, while it was good to hear her sister being more like her normal happy self, Vicky resented that laugh on a personal level.

'He knows of a job going in Kinbrae.'

'What as? Kinbrae's tiny. Who could possibly be wanting a nurse?'

'The GP practice.'

That made her sister think.

'Ah. Well, that's good. Kinbrae's not very far away. It would be lovely if you got a job there. I'd love for you to be closer — and not only because you're handy in a crisis.'

Despite still being annoyed, Vicky laughed.

'Well, being closer to you would be a definite advantage. Though there are no guarantees I'll even get an interview. I imagine there will be tons of applicants.'

* * *

Ryan was waiting for her in the bar around the corner from Claire's house. She saw him straight away as he stood up and waved.

'I've brought my purse this time,' she announced as she arrived at his table in the corner. 'What can I get for you?'

'No, I'll get these.'

'Wouldn't hear of it. Not only are you helping me out, but I owe you for rescuing me from a potentially embarrassing situation with the tea earlier.'

'OK, if you insist.' He sat back down and asked for a beer and she went to order their drinks.

This would keep things on a friendly footing, she decided. Her insistence on paying for the round would send him the message she didn't see this as any kind of date. And that was important. She didn't think he'd ever found out about the giant crush she'd had on him as a teenager — and she very much wanted to keep it that way.

'So.' She put their drinks down and sat opposite him. 'Tell me about this job.'

Ryan took a quick drink and then launched into what could only be described as a sales pitch.

'Are you on commission?' she asked with a laugh.

'No.' He looked a little sheepish. 'But I feel kind of responsible for Josh being in this fix. He'd asked if I was interested when the post was vacant a while back. I wasn't, but I recommended Elise. And now she's leaving.'

'That's not your fault.'

He shrugged.

'Not exactly. But Josh is a friend, so I'd like to help him out.'

'How do you know I'd be any good? I might be a terrible nurse and it might end really badly. How would that leave your friendship with Dr Carter then?'

His blue eyes burned into hers and the world seemed to stop spinning.

'Are you a terrible nurse, Vicky?'

'Well, no. As it happens I'm an excellent nurse. But you couldn't have known that.'

He smiled into her eyes and she felt the hint of an upward curve on her own lips.

'I knew,' he said quietly.

'But how could you?'

'Gut instinct.'

She shook her head to try to free herself of the intimate feel of the situation.

'Besides,' he added. 'Josh will be looking for references — so if you did turn out to be terrible, it would all be his own fault.'

She smiled at him over the rim of her glass and was startled by the expression that crossed his face. It was only there for a moment, but it held her spellbound. And she knew she hadn't been mistaken.

Although maybe it wasn't so strange. It was probably a look of surprise she'd noticed: that had to be the first time she'd genuinely smiled — and meant it — since she'd arrived back in Aberbrig.

* * *

Ryan's breath caught when Vicky smiled at him like that. Only for a moment, but he suspected it could mean trouble if he wasn't careful.

'Would you like another?' he asked, nodding at her empty glass and forcing himself to speak as normally as possible.

'Thank you, but I'd better not. I need to get back to see how Claire's doing. That's the reason I'm back here in Aberbrig, after all.'

'OK.' He finished the last of his own drink and got to his feet. 'I'll walk you back.'

'There's no need. It's only around the corner — I'll be fine.'

'It's on my way,' he said and they fell into step beside each other.

For some reason he wanted to prolong this meeting, even though he had no interest in exploring the idea that she could be important in his life. Maybe if they'd run into each other like this in five or ten years it might have been different. But not now. Not when he wasn't ready for anything more than the most light-hearted of relationships.

At least he'd recognised what might happen at a time when he could put a stop to it.

He had to give himself full marks for that.

'Let me know how you get on with Josh,' he said. 'Do you have a pen? I'll give you my mobile number. You can text me.'

'Of course.' She bent her head to look in her bag for a pen and paper. He marvelled at how tiny she was. Even standing on the first of the steps that led to her sister's front door, she barely reached his shoulder.

'OK,' she said, emerging triumphantly from her bag with her pen and a notebook. 'Ready.' He told her the number and he watched as she wrote it down in neat blue ink.

She was like a fragile, beautiful doll. No wonder he felt a worrying urge to take care of her.

4

Kinbrae Calling

Faye and the other nurses were out when he arrived back at the house. He put the kettle on and cut himself a large slice of his mother's plum cake. Then he phoned Josh to let him know to expect Vicky's call.

'What's she like?' Josh asked quite reasonably.

'Lovely,' he said, then could have bitten his tongue. He knew he'd given himself away when Josh chuckled softly.

'I meant as a nurse.'

'I have it on good authority that she's an excellent nurse,' he said, repeating what she'd told him. 'She's got experience working in hospitals and GP practices. And she can provide references. I think you'll be impressed.'

'What's she doing now?'

'Working for an agency while she's looking for a permanent job.'

'So, she could start soon.' There was a thoughtful silence. 'Well, that's certainly a point in her favour,' the doctor said. 'The last time I advertised there wasn't a single applicant — which is very hard to believe when jobs are so thin on the ground. But I suppose nobody wants to work this far out of town. I'll set up a meeting with Vicky as soon as possible.'

* * *

A few days later, Vicky couldn't believe how nervous she was. Her hands shook as she straightened the lapels of the jacket from the silver-grey skirt suit she'd borrowed from her sister.

'You look fab,' Claire told her.

'Thanks for letting me borrow this.' She glanced away from her reflection in the mirror and cast her sister a nervous little smile. 'It didn't even cross my mind to pack for an interview. I've only brought jeans and tops.'

'Just as well we're roughly the same size,' Claire said. 'The skirt's a bit loose and a tiny bit too long, but it will do — especially if you keep the jacket on. Now, are you sure you don't need me to come with you?'

Vicky shook her head.

'No, thank you. I'll be fine. Besides, you need to go and see your husband.'

Claire ginned. The worried air from only a few days ago had left her now that Steven was so much better. He was still in a lot of pain, of course, but mentally more himself.

'Got to make the most of my last free day,' she smiled in agreement. 'I've told Jack I'll be back at work tomorrow.'

Which meant it was just as well Vicky had a job interview. She would rattle around this house with nothing to do all day and her sister at her own work.

Josh was lovely and put her at ease immediately. In his early thirties, he was dedicated and passionate about his work — everything anyone could wish a doctor to be.

'Are you likely to take off at any time soon?' he asked kindly as he perused her curriculum vitae.

'I can't rule it out,' she told him honestly. 'I love living and working in Edinburgh and I do want to go back there. But, for the foreseeable future I need to be around here, to support my sister and to help with my brother-in-law.'

She quickly explained the circumstances of Steven's accident.

He nodded sympathetically.

'Yes, I can see why your sister will need your help.'

She got the job. She could barely believe it. And Josh agreed to a temporary contract. Though he made it clear he was looking for a permanent nurse.

The euphoria of being wanted and the convenience of the post's proximity to Aberbrig far outweighed her misgivings of being tied to an area that held sad memories.

Maybe she was growing up at last she reflected, as she tottered along Kinbrae

High Street in Claire's high heels. She liked the stature and the air of confidence they lent her, but she didn't think she'd ever work out how to move elegantly in them.

To prove the point, she stumbled and twisted her ankle as she passed the café.

Glancing through the window, she saw a couple of the tables occupied, but plenty of free ones, too. And it looked warm and cosy in there. Giving a shiver in the late afternoon breeze, she went in.

Paula was chatting to two ladies who looked as though they might be twins. She glanced up and smiled as Vicky walked through the door.

'Excuse me, please, Joyce, Alice,' she said to the women, then walked towards Vicky. 'How did it go?' she asked with a smile.

'How did what go?'

'The interview. Please tell me you got the job?'

Vicky felt her jaw drop.

'How did you know?'

58

Paula laughed.

'No such thing as secrets around here. You should know that.' Then she laughed again at Vicky's expression. 'Claire phoned me,' she confided, putting Vicky out of her misery. 'She wanted to let me know how Steven was doing and she mentioned you were on your way to Kinbrae.'

'I got the job,' she shared with a grin. And Paula gave a cry of delight, earning her a glare of disapproval from one of the ladies she'd been speaking to and a smile from the other.

'Sit down,' Paula instructed. 'We must celebrate. Cake for everyone,' she cried as she looked around the café to her handful of customers. Then she went behind the counter and picked out what had to be the most delicious-looking treat Vicky had ever seen. 'Dark chocolate cake with a raspberry buttercream filling, and dark chocolate frosting,' she said with an air of triumph as she began to cut generous slices for everyone.

'Thank you.' Vicky accepted her plate eagerly and dived in with her fork. The confection looked as fluffy as a cloud and Vicky doubted any human hand could have baked anything so light. 'Did you make this?' she asked Paula incredulously.

'I wish,' Paula said with feeling. 'No, I'm afraid I don't bake. This is the work of my future mother-in-law: Heather McGregor.'

Vicky was impressed. And she could see what all the fuss was about at last. Her peers, when she'd been at school, had often taken the bus to Kinbrae for tea at McGregor's. At the time she'd thought that Heather's sons, who worked part-time in the café as teenagers, had been the attraction. But now she thought there might have been more to it. And she suddenly felt she'd missed out.

'I'll order a piece of this to take away, please,' she said between mouthfuls. 'I think Claire would appreciate it.' She thought for a moment. 'Do you think it would be greedy if I took another slice for myself, too?'

Paula laughed.

'It would be sensible. Imagine how you'd feel having to watch your sister tuck in while you just sat there.'

She smiled, able to see why Paula was so good at running the café — she obviously appreciated her merchandise and knew her customers well. Even new customers who were visiting for the first time.

'I'll have to watch it,' Vicky said as she paid Paula for the takeaway cake. 'You're too handy for the surgery here. I'll be the size of an elephant if I'm not careful.'

Paula burst into laughter.

'It would take a lot of cake to make someone as tiny as you look like an elephant.'

Vicky felt almost happy as she made her way back to the car, her cake box safely in her arms. Everything was falling into place. Almost as if it was meant to be.

Ryan had been waiting all afternoon for a call or a text from Vicky. As time dragged on, he assumed she must have forgotten about him. He was alarmed at how flat that thought made him feel. He was considering phoning the surgery to speak to Josh when the doorbell rang.

He blinked when he saw a tiny blonde woman on his doorstop. Then she turned and smiled and his heart flipped. She was wearing a smart business suit that seemed slightly too big — the long sleeves and wide shoulders making her seem even smaller than she usually was.

'How did it go?' He held his breath. He was pretty sure Josh would have made an offer — he would have to be daft not to. But, until he knew for certain, there was still that element of doubt. And it suddenly mattered very much that Vicky would have a reason to stay around. Something to tie her to the place.

'I tried to ring you as soon as I got back to the car, but I must have written your number down wrong because I couldn't get through.'

She hadn't forgotten him after all. He was overwhelmed by something that might have been pure joy.

'Well?' he prompted, eager to hear her news.

'I got it.'

She grinned and he swooped down and lifted her clean off the ground. He couldn't understand afterwards what had come over him. But at the time it had seemed like the right thing to do.

Her breath was warm on his neck and for a moment he didn't want to put her down.

Luckily she was still smiling when he did.

'I'm sorry,' he said. 'I shouldn't have done that. But well done! That's fabulous news.'

'I'm pretty chuffed.' She grinned again.

'I can see that. Would you like to come in? I'm about to start on dinner. How about you join me to celebrate?' He couldn't believe he'd asked her to join him again. What was happening to him? She didn't look too sure in any case and he felt a huge surge of disappointment. 'Or do you have to get back?'

'I'd best get back.' She gave a little shrug. 'I need to tell Claire about the job.'

And despair turned to joy as he realised that, if she was yet to see her sister, the first thing she'd done when she'd returned to Aberbrig was to come to see him.

'Before you go,' he said, 'would you like me to put my number into your phone?'

She bit her lip and looked at him uncertainly.

'Just in case there's every anything I can help with,' he added, suddenly feeling very foolish and experiencing the need to explain himself.

Her expression cleared and she smiled.

'Thank you, that's really kind.' She handed her phone over and their fingers brushed — and his breath caught.

Really, he knew he should just walk away. He'd done his bit. If she needed help of any sort, Claire had a whole network of friends and in-laws Vicky could call on. But he still found himself keying in his number and saving it. And, even while he hoped she would never be in difficulties, he did hope she might find a reason to call him soon.

★   ★   ★

Vicky spent the next few days preparing for taking over as practice nurse at Kinbrae surgery. Elise was leaving the following week and Josh wanted them to double up for the final few days. But that meant Vicky had a week to get herself sorted out in terms of moving back to Aberbrig.

'You'll stay here with me and Steven,

of course,' Claire said.

'If you're sure you don't mind,' Vicky accepted gratefully.

If she had somewhere to stay then at least she could cross flat hunting off her 'to do' list. And she'd be here during the difficult weeks after Steven's discharge when Claire would really need her close at hand.

He wouldn't be out for a while yet, though, and Claire was back at work and more like her usual self, so Vicky took the opportunity of that free week to head back to Edinburgh. She needed to fetch more clothes for one thing. And she needed to see her flatmates.

She flirted with the idea of giving the room up — after all, it was daft to pay rent for a place she wasn't going to be using for months. But she liked her flatmates and she needed to know that she had somewhere to stay when she was able to go back to her real life.

'I'll be back as soon as I can,' she promised Kerry and Rachel, the two nurses she shared with. 'And I've arranged for my rent to be paid by direct debit.'

They both thoroughly hugged her. And she knew she was doing the right thing holding on to the room; good flatmates were difficult to find.

The girls took her out for a drink that night. She knew she should have been sorting through her things and deciding what to take, but saying goodbye was more important. Especially if she wanted good friends to come back to.

$$\star \quad \star \quad \star$$

She took the drive to Aberbrig at a leisurely pace this time. Now she wasn't worried about exactly what she'd find on her arrival, she relaxed and enjoyed the views as she counted down the miles.

It was a very different prospect now. And the dread in her heart at the thought of going back wasn't as intense as it had been last time. Staying with Claire for those days after Steven's accident had made Vicky see that things had changed. Yes, the memories had been there — and probably always would be. But sometimes it was nice to remember, even if the experience was bittersweet.

Her life was no longer there, she was in no doubt about that. For the first time since moving away, however, she could hope that once Steve was recovered and she returned to Edinburgh, she would be able to visit her sister in Aberbrig now and then.

Claire was at work when Vicky arrived. So she started to heave the first bag out of the car and instantly wished she hadn't crammed so much in.

'Need a hand?'

Ryan McGregor.

Her heart gave a little leap. She told it sternly to calm down, made sure her smile wasn't overly enthusiastic, and turned around.

'That's so kind. Thank you.' She knew she could have managed; after all, she'd taken these same bags down to the car from her flat in Edinburgh by herself. But if a strong, handsome man was offering to help, the job would be finished much faster.

She handed him her car keys.

'There's another one and a backpack in the back,' she said with a smile and he grinned back. 'If you could lock the car after you've brought them in, I'll go and put the kettle on.'

She was inordinately pleased that she'd bumped into Ryan. Whatever she told herself, or Claire, she still had a soft spot for him.

But the fact remained that she was not likely to stay in Aberbrig long-term. So there was no point giving in to the temptation to grow closer to him.

She'd been in a similar position before and it had ended badly. And, if nothing else, Vicky prided herself on always learning from past mistakes. She would have to be jolly sure of a man before handing him her heart again. And, unfortunately, she wasn' staying around long enough to find c what kind of man Ryan McGregor was.

* * *

Ryan took the bags inside. They were heavy and he wondered at how someone as tiny and slight as Vicky had hoped to manage on her own. He could only assume she must be stronger than she looked.

'I've missed you about the place,' he told her as he sat down at Claire's kitchen table and waited for her to bring the tea over.

'I've only been gone a few days.' She laughed and her pale complexion turned a delightful pink.

'It's always good to see a friendly face about the place,' he added, to prevent her getting the wrong impression from his candid confession. Or perhaps it was the right impression, even if he didn't really want it to be. He had missed her, after all. And there were certain conclusions to be drawn from that.

'So,' she said as she poured the tea. 'What's been going on while I've been away?'

'Just the usual. Work's been busy, as it always is. And we're bracing ourselves for an even busier winter. But that's nothing out of the ordinary. What about you? Where have you been and what have you been up to?'

'I went to sort things out with my flat in Edinburgh. Tie up loose ends.'

Well, he hadn't been expecting that. It seemed she planned to stay in Aberbrig, which would be good news for Josh.

And good news for you, too, a little voice inside his head nagged.

'You gave up your place?'

She shook her head.

'Not exactly. But I told my flatmate I'd be away for a while. I won't be goin: back until Steven's properly on his fee

He was disappointed, he could: pretend otherwise. The thought of Vi leaving wasn't a pleasant one.

5

First Day

Vicky was nervous about her first day at the surgery.

'Don't be silly,' she told her reflection sternly. 'You've got years of experience. It will all be fine.' Besides, she was only shadowing Elise for the first couple of days, so it was hardly likely she'd be thrown in above her head.

Josh was getting out of his car as she drove into the car park. He waited while she found a space and locked her Mini up.

'Ready for the big day?' he asked as she approached.

She took a deep breath.

'As ready as I'll ever be.'

He laughed.

'There's nothing to be worried about,' he promised her. 'Doreen hasn't booked too many patients for you today. She thought you'd need a bit of space to find your feet — and time for Elise to explain our procedures to you.'

She didn't know who Doreen was, but she took an immediate liking to the sound of her.

'I take it Doreen's the receptionist?'

'One of them. She job-shares with her daughter Sophie.'

Sophie was on duty today. And Vicky liked her, too.

'I love it here,' she said with a grin when Vicky asked. 'And the hours are great — they fit in with school time for my twins.'

'How old are your children?'

'Five.' She smiled. 'They just started school this year.'

They chatted for a few minutes about Sophie's family and then Elise arrived and introduced herself.

'It's a lovely place to work,' the other nurse told her. 'I'm going to miss it.'

Elise showed her around the surgery. It didn't take long — there was much of it to see. Vicky wondered at the difference between this tiny, converted bungalow and the purpose-built London surgery she had worked in. The London one had all mod cons, but this one had character. She liked the feel of the place.

'And I've saved the best until last. This is your treatment room,' Elise said as she finished off the tour.

'Erm, it's cosy.' The room was tiny, with a computer, desk, two patient chairs and an examination bed crammed in.

Elise laughed.

'That's one way to put it. There are a few minutes before the first patient arrives, so we'll bring in a chair for you. Then we can get you logged into the computer and I'll show you where all the supplies are.'

The first few days went swimmingly. Vicky was impressed at the range of treatments she was expected to deal with. If only this job had been in 'dinburgh it would have been perfect.

Elise did a thorough job of handing

over. So much so that by the following week, when Vicky was expected to cope alone, her nerves had been long forgotten.

When that first patient arrived, Vicky was a little alarmed to see she was wearing the biggest frown in history.

A quick glance at the computer screen confirmed the lady's name — Vicky didn't want to risk further displeasure by accidentally getting that wrong.

'Good morning, Miss Imrie,' she said brightly. 'How can I help you today?'

Miss Imrie regarded her coldly for a moment then she held out her hand.

'I cut myself with a kitchen knife last week,' she said. 'Elise said I was to come in and have the dressing changed.'

It took Vicky a few moments to locate the right dressings.

'Sorry about that,' she said brightly. 'First day on my own. But I'll know where they are next time.'

Miss Imrie didn't look amused and

Vicky decided it was probably better to get on with the job rather than try to make polite chat.

Thankfully, the rest of her patients that morning were a little friendlier. But she still couldn't shake the feeling that Miss Imrie hadn't been impressed with her.

'Why the frown?' Paula asked at lunchtime when Vicky popped into the café for her break.

'Aw, it's nothing, really.' She smiled, pleased to see Paula's friendly face. 'Only wondering how long it will take before some of the patients accept I'm there to help and I know what I'm doing.'

Paula laughed.

'You're talking about Joyce Imrie?' she suggested.

Vicky shifted uncomfortably in her chair. Patient confidentiality meant she couldn't confirm or deny Paula's suspicion.

'It's OK,' Paula assured her. 'I know you can't say, but she told me she was going to see you. So I've added two and two.' She smiled. 'Take no notice of what she says. She likes to have a good old grumble, but she's OK, really.'

Vicky smiled, grateful for the reassurance, but determined not to indulge in gossip about a patient.

'What's the soup of the day?' she asked.

'Broccoli and Stilton. Freshly made on the premises this morning by Heather.'

'Sounds good,' she said. 'I'll have a bowl, please.'

The soup was lovely. As was the triple chocolate muffin Vicky had for afters. Although she promised herself that sort of thing would only be for special occasions — like a celebration of her first proper day.

'Hope to see you again,' Paula called as Vicky got up to go back to work.

'I'm sure you will,' she replied. 'You're way too handy for the surgery. I'll mostly likely be in here for my lunch every day.'

When she got back to Claire's that night, the place was in darkness. Her sister must have gone to the hospital to see Steven.

Vicky was tempted to turn on the TV and slouch on the sofa, but she was still buzzing with the newness of her first day flying solo as the practice nurse at Kinbrae Surgery. She guessed she would be too restless to settle. Besides, she hadn't done any proper exercise since she'd arrived here; she hadn't even thought to bring her kit when Claire had phoned originally.

But she had everything she needed now, after her recent trip to fetch her things. So she put on her running gear and headed down towards the sea front.

It was pretty quiet down there at this time in the evening; most people would have only just come in from work, and were probably relaxing with their families.

Solitude suited Vicky fine and she

broke into a run, breathing the fresh salty air deeply into her lungs. The breeze had taken on the chill of the water, but she soon warmed up as her feet pounded the pavement.

The first she knew that there was someone running alongside her was when she heard his voice suddenly.

'How was your first day at the surgery?'

She stifled the urge to let out a panicked scream.

'Ryan. You frightened me half to death.'

'Sorry.' His teeth flashed white in the gloomy evening light as he grinned. 'I didn't mean to sneak up on you, but it's hard to make much noise in trainers.'

She glanced at his clothing — he was also dressed for a run and they jogged along together quite comfortably.

'Have you been working?' she asked.

'Not yet, but I'm due there soon,' he replied. 'I'm only just out of my bed, so this is a wake up; fresh air and exercise. I always find dropping off to sleep

— and waking up — more difficult when I'm on night shift.' They ran a few metres in silence. 'So, how was your day?'

'Yes, fine. I think I'm going to like it there.'

He grinned again. She liked it when he smiled.

'That's good to hear. Does that mean you might think about staying around here?'

Her smile faded.

'I'll stay as long as Claire needs me, of course. And I think that will be quite a while.'

'But afterwards?' he persisted.

'When Steven's recovered . . . ' She took a deep breath as they jogged along. 'When Steven's recovered, I'll go back to my real life.'

Although, she was finding more and more that Aberbrig wasn't quite the miserable place she remembered from her teens.

She sent a quiet smile winging Ryan's way and her stomach flipped when he smiled back.

Yes, the place had definitely improved.

'How does Josh feel about your plans?'

She shrugged.

'He knows I'm only here temporarily. He'll find someone else when the time comes.'

* * *

Ryan sometimes played football with a local team, but it was difficult to always fit the training in with his shifts. So, running had become a means to an end; a way to keep fit that was readily available on his doorstep and that didn't have the hefty price tag associated with a swanky gym.

But these days it was fast becoming his favourite pastime.

He and Vicky started to meet up so they could run together. And it was amazing how much fun it was to run with a friend.

Though he did wonder how wise he

was being when he found himself looking forward to the next run just so he could spend time with her. And when he found himself looking at her and wondering what it might be like to kiss her.

Then, one night, just as he was about to set off, his mobile rang.

He glanced quickly at the display and smiled as he answered the call.

'Hi, Vicky.'

'Hello.' Her soft voice seemed to reach down the phone and caress his skin.

He smiled again. He seemed to be smiling a lot these days.

'Have you looked out in the last few minutes?'

He hadn't, but he didn't really need to. He could hear the howling of the wind and the rain beating at his window. It didn't take much imagination to know what it would be like outside.

'Don't tell me you're going to let a bit of rain put you off our run?' he teased.

She laughed.

'A bit of rain? It looks like someone has upturned a bucket of water over us.'

He twitched the curtains aside and had to concede that, indeed, that was exactly what it looked like.

'I'm up for it if you are,' he said, not quite wanting to let go of the idea of seeing her tonight.

'I've a better idea,' she said. 'Claire's at the hospital for the next few hours, so why don't you come around here and I'll cook you some dinner. It's about time I thanked you properly for mentioning my name to Josh.'

He laughed.

'How many times are you going to thank me for that?'

'Do you want dinner or not?'

'I want dinner.'

'Good. I'll see you here in five minutes.'

There was no point taking the car as Claire's house was so close to his own, so he found his waterproof jacket. pulled the hood up and ran for it.

He dripped rainwater over Claire's tiled hallway as he took the jacket off.

'Difficult to look good in an anorak,' he joked.

'I don't know. I think you'd look good in anything.'

He looked over at her in surprise, just in time to find her blue eyes widen and mirror his shocked response. And as a delicious soft pink tone warmed her skin, he found he was smiling at her.

'I meant to say that if you give me your coat I'll hang it by the Aga so it dries.' She blushed even harder and he resisted the urge that would have seen his grin widen. He grinned way too much around her.

Their fingers brushed as she took his coat and then she disappeared into the kitchen, reappearing moments later without his coat, but with two glasses of wine. She handed him one.

'Our meal's nearly ready,' she said. 'Let's go into the living room while we wait. You're not in a hurry are you?'

'Not at all,' he said. 'Night off tonight. Dinner can take as long as it likes.'

There was a fire roaring in the sitting room and it all looked very cosy. It seemed natural that he sit next to her on the sofa and his arm easily rested along the back. It would be so simple to move it so it was around her shoulders.

And the thought of doing that didn't frighten him. It was that kind of night — a night when a person should be in a warm living room, with their arm around a beautiful girl.

But he guessed it was too soon in their relationship for that kind of manoeuvre. And possibly it would always be too soon. She had plans to leave once her brother-in-law was better, after all.

And he had plans not to get involved in any serious relationships for the foreseeable future. Settling down was at least five years in the future for him.

'I'm afraid it's only pasta,' she said she served up at the dining room ta' a short while later.

'Pasta's fine,' he assured her. And it was. 'It's delicious,' he said between mouthfuls.'

She smiled across at him, but she didn't say anything and they ate the rest of their meal in an easy silence.

'I bought in pudding,' she admitted as though it was a guilty secret. 'I dropped by Paula's café on the way home. She said this was one of your mum's creations.' She put a box containing a couple of slices of gateau on the table and fetched plates. 'I feel a bit odd inviting you over to eat food your own mother made.'

'I've no complaints about that.'

'No. I don't think many people would complain about a Heather McGregor cake.' She smiled as she served the gateau.

'Was it raining in Kinbrae when you left?' It had only started here just before her phone call.

'Er, no. But it was cold and 'serable.'

'So skiving from our running date was premeditated.'

She blushed again.

'Perhaps.' She looked at him with innocent-looking blue eyes. 'A girl gets tired of running,' she said. 'I thought it was time we did something else.'

'So if it hadn't rained you would have asked me over in any case?'

'If I had, would you have come?'

He looked into her lovely face and felt his heart rate soar.

'Absolutely.'

He held her gaze and there was no denying something passed between them. He had no idea how long they sat there like that. But eventually she looked away.

'I should do something about these dishes,' she said. 'And get us some coffee.'

He got up to help her tidy up.

'You don't need to do that,' she said. 'You're a guest.'

'If I help it means I get to spend more time with you,' he told her quite reasonably.

She didn't make any further objection and he took that as a good sign. Although, spending time together didn't necessarily mean anything more than that, he told himself. Neither of them was looking for something long-term; they were good friends at the very most.

'Shall we take these through to the living room?' she asked as she put their coffees and some mints on a tray.

'Good idea.'

This time he did take the opportunity to put his arm around her shoulders and as she snuggled up against him on the sofa, in front of the fire and with the rain beating against the window, it occurred to him that he could stay here like this for a very long time.

*   *   *

Vicky heard someone calling her name. As she surfaced from a deep sleep, she was aware of someone shifting at her side, moving his arms from around her.

Bleary-eyed, she sat up and blinked.

'You two looked very cosy fast asleep there,' Claire commented.

Vicky was mortified. To be caught fast asleep on the sofa, in the arms of a man she had sworn she most definitely wasn't interest in, was embarrassing to say the least. Particularly when the person doing the catching was the very sister she had done the swearing to.

Ryan wasn't in the least ruffled, though.

'We've both had a busy week,' he told her. 'How's Steven?'

Claire nodded.

'They're talking about him coming home soon,' she said with an air of quiet excitement. 'I can't wait to have him back.'

'That's good news,' Ryan told her.

'It is,' Vicky agreed, smiling broadly. 'The best.'

Ryan was pleased, of course he was. But he realised what this news meant: Steven was getting better and Vicky would be leaving Aberbrig soon.

Just as well he'd decided he was only looking for friendship. But even as he tried to convince himself of that, the thought of not seeing her about the place wasn't a pleasant one.

6

Steven's Homecoming

'Now the real work begins,' Ryan told Vicky when he popped round to help her set the dining room up as a bedroom for Steven. With his injuries, it would be a while before he could successfully negotiate stairs and it made sense that he was downstairs as it would make things easier for Claire and Vicky as they looked after him.

'It does, indeed,' Vicky replied.

She and Claire had spoken about how they would work things. Vicky's job at the surgery meant that she wouldn't be around much during the weekdays. But Claire had arranged to work from home so she would be here to look after her husband.

Vicky was to take over in the evenings, to give Claire a chance to catch up on any work she hadn't been able to manage during the day. And, also, so she could occasionally have some time to herself.

This would mean less free time for Vicky.

'I won't be able to meet you as often,' she said. And she hated the tiny catch in her voice that gave away more than she'd have liked.

He folded her up in his arms and hugged her tight. She rested against him; his scent tickled at her nose and his warmth made her feel safe.

'We'll still see each other,' he said. 'I'll make sure of that.' And, despite her protestations of not wanting to fall for Ryan, she was comforted by his assurance. And by his arms still holding her tight.

Bad idea, a voice inside her head cried. *You're not staying around here for long. And he's Ryan McGregor. The popular boy from your school days you have no business falling for.*

Reluctantly, she drew away and

offered him an apologetic smile.

'We'd better get this room sorted out so Claire can bring her husband home.' She did her best to sound cheerful so he wouldn't guess at the turmoil his hug had stirred up.

He gave a short nod. But she couldn't help noticing he was pale and distracted.

They worked in silence for a few moments before he spoke again.

'Still enjoying the surgery?' he asked as he heaved the mattress onto its base.

'Very much,' she replied, throwing a sheet over the newly-repositioned bed and starting to tuck it in. 'Although, with Paula's café on the doorstep, the weight's piling on.'

He grabbed a corner of the sheet and she gasped as their eyes met across the bed.

'You look fine to me.'

In that moment, something passed between them. Again. Something that had her heart almost beating out of her chest.

Her head swam. These moments were happening far too frequently for comfort.

'You must stop saying things like that,' she told him breathlessly.

'Things like what?'

'All these compliments. You'll have me believing you if you're not careful.'

'Why wouldn't you believe me? I'm deadly serious.'

Too charming by half. That was his problem. Charming enough to turn a girl's head. Even if that girl was sensible enough to know that he was out of her league.

Vicky was determined that what they shared was no more than a good friendship. No matter what being close to him might do to her heart rate. No matter how comfortably she'd slept in his arms on the sofa the other night. Men like Ryan didn't fall for girls like her. They went for girls who were outgoing and popular — like themselves.

She laughed nervously. She knew he

wasn't making fun of her, but she also knew there was no way he could truly be interested in her. Not in a romantic sense, at least.

And she had to remember that. Because, suddenly, the fact she wasn't going to be in the area long didn't seem enough to protect her heart.

★   ★   ★

When Steven arrived home, Ryan was still at the house and he stayed long enough to get the patient settled.

'I'm lucky to have two highly trained professionals at my service,' he joked weakly as they helped him into bed.

'Told you when they brought you into the General that we'd take care of you, didn't I?' Ryan said brightly.

But Steven looked blank.

'I don't remember.' He chewed his lip and frowned, trying to think. 'Were you there that day?'

'Don't worry about it,' Ryan said. 'All you need to know is that you're going to be fine.'

Steven was still on strong pain medication and was tired after the short journey home.

'Rest now,' Vicky told him gently.

'I want to stay with him for a while,' Claire said. 'I can't believe he's home.' Steven looked up at her and the tenderness in his eyes made Vicky want to cry. She knew that Claire and Steven were very lucky to have found each other.

She felt a sudden sadness that she didn't have anyone special in her own life. And her gaze fluttered unnervingly towards Ryan, before she glanced back towards the patient.

'I'll be in soon to make sure you're OK,' she told Steven. Then she and Ryan left the room.

'Thank you so much for coming over to help today,' she said to him as he shrugged into his jacket and prepared to leave. 'I'd never had managed to move that bed downstairs without you.'

He grinned and her insides quivered.

'Pleasure.'

Then he bent his head and brushed his lips against hers in the merest breath of a butterfly kiss goodbye.

'See you soon,' he promised.

The effect of that brief kiss lingered long after he'd gone. She longed to talk about it, to analyse what it might mean, with her sister. But the urge to keep it to herself was stronger –– to hug the memory and savour the knowledge it had happened without Claire reading too much into it.

Because she was pretty sure, deep down, that it hadn't meant anything. As kisses went, it had been very casual. And the only way it could have been less personal was if he'd pecked her on the cheek. Or kissed her forehead as though she was his gran.

★ ★ ★

With a sigh, Vicky settled down with her coffee and picked up her magazine. Claire was at work today; she'd been needed at the office. As it had been a quiet afternoon at the surgery, Josh had agreed Vicky could take a few hours off in case Steven needed her.

He was asleep at the moment, which she was glad of; her brother-in-law, who had never said a cross word in her hearing before, had transformed into the grumpiest of patients since he'd arrived home.

Not that it was surprising — it was often the case with very active people that when they were laid low they found it difficult to cope with enforced inactivity. And Steven had been sporty. He'd played football, tennis, and badminton in his spare time. Not to mention his habit of climbing onto the tops of buildings daily for his work.

She turned the page and began to read an article on the benefits of a good night's sleep. She'd only read the first paragraph when there was a crash followed by a loud cry for help from the new bedroom.

Putting down her coffee and throwing the magazine to one side, she ran through to what had so recently been the dining room to find Steven on the floor.

'Oh no. What happened? Are you OK?'

'Stupid leg,' he muttered. 'I thought I'd manage to hop through to the wet room, but it gave way.'

She knew there was no point in telling him off. This had been a lesson, she was sure — falling to the floor wasn't an experience he would want to repeat in a hurry. So she kept the rebuke that hovered on her tongue to herself.

She quickly checked him over as he lay on the floor and it seemed he'd been very lucky. His fall had caused no further damage as far as she could tell.

'I'm going to have to call for help,' she said. 'I won't be able to lift you back onto the bed by myself.'

Luckily, she happened to know it was Ryan's day off. She didn't stop to think why he was the first person who popped into her mind when she needed help; she called him without a moment's hesitation.

He was over in five minutes.

Steven allowed him to help, though he wasn't happy about it.

'Hate not being able to do things for myself,' he muttered.

'You'll be back to normal in no time,' Ryan assured him.

'But I don't like that I have to have help to do everything.'

'We're all vulnerable at some time,' Vicky told him as she plumped up the pillows around him. 'Just be grateful that you will mend. Some people aren't so lucky.'

He nodded.

'I know.'

'Everyone missed you at football,' Ryan said, taking a seat. The two men began to discuss the sport, moving easily from the local team they both belonged to and on to a discussion of their favourite team that happened to be doing quite well this season.

Vicky left them to it. Her coffee was stone cold by the time she went back to it, so she went to make a fresh pot. Putting cups, a jug of milk and a bowl of sugar onto a tray, she took them through to Ryan and Steven. They were still deep in conversation.

'Thanks,' Steven muttered as she laid a cup of coffee at the side of his good arm.

She handed Ryan his drink and their hands brushed. She felt a tingle in her fingers and stifled a gasp.

Looked like he was unaffected, though.

'Thank you,' he said, barely looking in her direction.

She was being daft, she knew she was. She knew he looked on her as a friend. But she didn't feel like hanging around when Ryan was so indifferent to her presence.

Vicky had long since gone back to her own coffee and her magazine when Claire arrived home.

'How is he?' Claire asked.

'He's OK now. Ryan's in with him, they're talking about sport.'

'What do you mean he's OK now?' There was panic in Claire's voice. 'What happened?'

Vicky grimaced.

'Let's just say he now knows he can't expect too much too soon. He tried to get out of bed.'

Claire didn't look amused. She stormed through to the bedroom and Vicky followed in her wake. She was pleased now she hadn't said anything to Steven about how foolish he'd been; it looked as though the poor man was about to get the telling off of his life from his wife.

'What do you think you were trying to do?' she ranted at him, fear for his well-being making her voice sharp. 'Are you trying to finish the job the fall started on you?'

It was a mark of how much Ryan's visit had lifted Steven's spirits that he was able to smile at his wife.

'I'm fine,' he told her mildly. 'I

overestimated my own abilities. But I won't make the same mistake again. Having to be lifted from the floor by one of my friends and a tiny slip of a sister-in-law is a big wake-up call.'

Claire let out a loud sigh.

'What am I going to do with you?'

'Why don't you come here and give me a kiss hello. I've missed you.'

Satisfied that all was well, Vicky put their empty cups onto the tray and took it back through to the kitchen.

'Thanks for the coffee.'

The back of her neck tingled as Ryan spoke right behind her. She didn't turn immediately, savouring the sensation of knowing he was so close. Slowly she rinsed the cups then loaded them into the dishwasher. Only then did she turn to face him.

He was only inches away. If she stood on her toes, she was sure she'd be able to feel his breath on her face.

She smiled.

'Thank you for coming to my rescue and rushing over to help.'

'Anytime. I've told you that. And I mean it.'

'I know.' She nodded.

'Now Claire's home, does that mean you're off duty here?'

'Yes. I'm planning a quiet afternoon with my magazine.' She smiled. Though she was tempted to ask him to stay and chat, she knew it was a bad idea.

He nodded and turned towards the door. His hand was on the handle when he hesitated and turned back to her. He seemed oddly shy for such a confidant man.

'Do you fancy coming out with me instead?' he asked.

7

Festive Plans

Ryan wasn't sure where that invitation had come from. He had no plans for this afternoon, so he had no idea where he could take her. But he knew he wanted to spend more time with her.

And he held his breath as he waited for her response. Which was odd in itself. Usually, if he suggested going out to a girl, it was never the end of the world if she refused. But somehow Vicky's answer seemed as though it might be.

Which set alarm bells ringing; he was swiftly getting himself involved in something he knew wasn't a good idea.

'What did you have in mind?' she asked.

'How about the art gallery, then a meal somewhere?' He was rather pleased with that suggestion. He suspected Vicky would enjoy the art gallery. And his brother, Mark, had an exhibition showing that he'd been meaning to see.

'I'll get my coat.'

And the tightness in his chest lifted and he felt he was able to breathe again.

They decided to walk around to the gallery. It was a lovely, crisp, autumnal day — the sky was a clear blue and the sun was shining, even if it was bitingly cold.

Her boots had heels of a couple of inches, but she still barely reached his shoulder and he had to make an effort to slow his normal walking pace so she didn't have to run to keep up with him.

He guided her towards Mark's exhibition and was pleased when she smiled.

'These are good,' she said as she took in the stunning seascapes and loch views his brother had created. 'Mark McGregor,' she read the artist's name.

'Your brother Mark?'

He nodded.

'I had no idea he could paint like this.'

'Nor did we for a long time,' he said. 'It was only when he left school and went to art college that any of us realised.'

Her blue eyes narrowed.

'I can't believe he wouldn't be telling everyone and anyone if he can paint like this.'

'He was worried he might not be able earn a living. For a long time it was a secret hobby — it was only when his art teacher encouraged him that he dared to think he could turn it into a profitable career.'

'In that case, I can understand why he was reluctant to share. It's important to know you can earn enough to get by. It was the need to earn a living that led me into nursing. Our parents didn't leave much and I couldn't live off Claire forever.'

'But you like nursing now?'

'Love it.' She moved on to the next painting; the sea from the beach at Aberbrig in the middle of a particularly spectacular storm. 'I couldn't imagine ever doing anything else.'

'Me neither.'

She looked up at him and they exchanged a look of mutual understanding. Ryan knew some of his colleagues thought of their work as just a job, but to him it was one of the most important occupations in the world. And it was obvious Vicky was on his wavelength.

'I remember Mark from school,' she said as they moved on to the next painting. 'He always seemed so studious. I had no idea all that seriousness hid the soul of an artist.'

'He's still serious.' Ryan laughed. 'Mum thinks that's how he manages to put so much intensity into his painting. In fact,' — Ryan slipped his arm around her waist and turned her around so they were facing. He needed to see her face — 'I was thinking of driving over to see Mum after we've eaten. I think she'd like to meet you.'

*　*　*

'I've already met Heather,' she laughed. Ryan's arm was still around her waist and being so close to him was making her light-headed. 'I have lunch in the café practically every day.'

'I mean I'd like to introduce you to her properly. Not as Claire's sister. And not as the new practice nurse in Kinbrae.'

She took a steadying breath as her heart began to race.

'What as, then?'

'My friend.'

This was too much to take in.

'Do you make a habit of introducing all your friends to your mum?'

He grinned.

'Not really. But I'd like you to meet her.'

She could be making a colossal fool of herself here, maybe mistaking his intentions. He was, after all, still Ryan McGregor. And she was still Vicky Simpson. Nothing much had changed in that respect. But, when he looked at her the way he was doing now, she could almost believe it could lead to more.

'I'm not going to be around here forever,' she said softly, as much to remind herself as it was to remind him.

His face clouded over.

'So you keep telling me. But I've been thinking about you a lot — ever since you ran into my arms at the hospital on the day they brought Steven in.'

She took a deep breath. 'What have you been thinking?'

His arm tightened around her; she could barely breathe.

'I know a relationship isn't what either of us wants at the moment, but I like you very much. And I think it would be daft to ignore what's between us.'

He was so close. She breathed in the

110

tangy scent of his aftershave; the urge to stand on her toes and press her lips against his was strong.

'I've been thinking about you, too. But I don't want to fall for you, Ryan. Not when I'm going to be leaving.'

Although she got the idea that it might already be too late to worry about that.

His lips brushed against hers and her toes tingled.

'Don't keep talking about leaving,' he said softly.

She looked up into his face, her heart beating madly.

'OK,' she agreed at last. 'Let's go see your mum.'

★ ★ ★

Vicky hadn't moved in the same circles as Ryan at school and had never imagined she would be invited to visit his home. Seeing the farmhouse where Ryan had grown up, where he would have played and run around with his two brothers, was a strange experience.

'It's a big house,' she said, looking out from the car as they drove into the yard. 'And look at all these lorries.'

'Dad has a haulage business,' he said.

'Yes, your mum mentioned that the other day when I was in Paula's café for lunch. I wasn't expecting to see so many vehicles parked outside the house, though.' She did a quick count — there were ten.

'Dad's worked hard to build the business up,' he said. 'The men clock off early on a Friday,' he went on as they walked towards the house. 'Always have — it's a tradition. That's why the trucks are all parked up.'

As he spoke, another lorry trundled into the yard and the driver got out. Vicky's eyes widened slightly when she saw it was a woman. And a slight, delicate-looking woman at that.

'Hi, Chrissy,' Ryan called.

Chrissy swung her auburn ponytail over her shoulder and smiled as she walked up to them.

'Hi, Ryan. Good to see you.'

Ryan introduced Chrissy to Vicky. 'Chrissy runs the office,' Ryan supplied.

Vicky felt her eyebrows lift to her hairline.

'And she drives lorries,' Vicky added dryly, glancing over her shoulder to the vehicle that Chrissy had only just gotten out of.

'I do indeed.' Chrissy laughed. 'But that's not strictly part of the job description. There were a couple of guys off sick today, so I stepped in to help.'

'Hey, you lot.' They were startled by Heather calling from the doorway. 'Are you going to stay out there all day, or are you coming inside?'

'We're just on our way in,' Ryan told her.

'Well hurry up. It's chilly out here,' she called as she turned to go back into the house. 'I'll go and put the kettle on.'

Chrissy went with them into the kitchen.

'How did the delivery go?' Denny

113

asked her from his armchair by the Aga.

'Fine,' Chrissy replied with a smile.

One look at Denny and Vicky could see straight away where the McGregor boys had got their red hair from. He was like an older, wearier version of Ryan. As that thought formed, the older man's eyes met hers and she smiled hesitantly.

'Mum, you've already met Vicky,' Ryan said and Heather nodded. He then turned to his dad. 'This is Vicky Simpson,' he told her father. 'A friend of mine.'

Denny got to his feet. He was only slightly shorter than his son and Vicky had to look up to make eye contact. He reached out a large, work-roughened hand and gave Vicky's a hearty shake.

'Good to meet you,' he said.

They were ushered over to sit around the scrubbed wooden kitchen table and Heather poured tea from a large brown teapot and cut generous slices of her homemade carrot cake.

'Help yourselves,' she invited as she

placed the cake in the centre of the table.

As Vicky sat there with her tea, nibbling on cake that was light as air, she felt a sudden and unexpected pang of grief. Ryan's family home was a happy one — even though she'd only been as far as the kitchen, she could feel it. And it reminded her so much of what she and Claire had lost when their parents had died.

Yes, she and her sister had each other. And she was grateful for that. But a huge part of their lives had been missing for the past few years. And that's why she had run away from Aberbrig — to try to escape from the emptiness that had plagued her.

'What's everyone doing for Christmas?' Heather's voice broke into her thoughts and she gave herself a mental shake and forced herself to put on a jolly expression.

'I'm working,' Ryan said.

'Poor you,' Chrissy said as she wrinkled her brow. 'I'm spending the day with Mum and my sister. I can't imagine how horrible it must be to work when you know everyone else is enjoying a holiday.'

Ryan's arm brushed against Vicky's as he shrugged a large shoulder.

'It's not so bad,' he said philosophically. 'There's always a good atmosphere at the hospital over Christmas. And someone has to work. There are still emergencies, even during the holidays.'

'What about you, Vicky?' Heather asked. 'Will you spend the day with Claire and Steven?'

Vicky was startled by the question. She hadn't thought as far as Christmas. But she should have — because it was only a matter of weeks away.

'I suppose I will,' she confirmed. 'I very much doubt Steven will have recovered enough for me to leave by then.'

She glanced across at Ryan and tried not to wince as she noticed his frown. She wished he wouldn't do that. It wasn't as though they were seriously seeing each other. And she'd been quite open in telling him she would only be here temporarily.

'And Hogmanay,' Denny added. 'Will you spend that with Claire and Steven, too?'

Vicky shrugged.

'We haven't made plans,' she admitted. 'But I suppose so.'

'You must come to us,' Heather told her. 'All three of you, if Steven's well enough to come out for a few hours. We normally have a bit of a party and it's always the more the merrier. Jack, Paula and Jess will be here. And Chrissy always joins us.'

'Wouldn't miss it for the world,' Chrissy said.

'Mark has said even he might make it this year. And Ryan won't be on duty if he's working over Christmas, so he'll be here, too.' Heather turned to her son. 'You can bring Vicky, can't you?'

Ryan glanced across at her and for a moment it seemed there was nobody else in the room.

'Do you want me to bring you?'

How could she refuse an offer like that?

Slowly, she nodded. And when Ryan grinned nothing else mattered.

As soon as they'd finished their tea, Ryan and Vicky got up to leave.

'Are you sure you won't you stay for something to eat?' Heather asked anxiously.

'We had a big meal before we came,' Ryan laughed. 'And you've fed us more than enough cake to keep us going until supper.'

Heather waved them off as they drove away and Ryan stopped the car on the lane once they were out of sight.

'I'm sorry,' he said. 'She fusses.'

'She's lovely,' Vicky said, meaning it. Then she frowned as she looked around. 'Why have we stopped?'

Ryan undid their seatbelts and leaned a little closer.

'The whole time we were in there, I couldn't stop thinking about getting you on your own.'

Suddenly she was breathless.

'Why?' her voice was disturbingly strange. She cleared her throat and then tried again. 'Why did you want to get me on my own?'

He grinned. He was leaning in so close now she could feel his breath on her face, and his gaze moved to her lips. He was going to kiss her. Ryan McGregor was going to kiss her. And, by the look on his face, she guessed it was about to get a whole lot more serious than the brief kisses they'd shared until now. If she could have travelled back in time her teenage self would have laughed in her own face at the very ridiculousness of the idea.

But now it was about to happen, nothing in the world made more sense.

He didn't answer. Instead he leaned forward a little more and when his lips met hers the kiss was the sweetest she'd ever known.

★　★　★

Ryan didn't know what it was about Vicky, but as the weeks flew by and he saw more of her, he couldn't imagine his life without her.

'What will you do Christmas night, after your shift's finished?' she asked him as they ran together along the seafront, early one morning exactly a week before Christmas Day.

It was a cold day, with frost thick on the ground and on the cars they passed. They had to tread carefully to avoid sliding all over the place. And it was still dark, the only light from the street-lamps overhead. If it hadn't been for the fact he was meeting her, Ryan would probably have given the run a miss.

He slowed his pace even more and ran his hand through his hair.

'Probably go home and open a can of soup.'

She grimaced.

'Won't you go and see your family?'

He shook his head.

'I'm on duty again on Boxing Day, so

it's best that I don't. Otherwise I'd be tempted to stay too long. Can't be bleary-eyed at work.'

She sighed softly.

'I don't like to think of you all alone at home on Christmas night.'

'I'll be fine. I'm a big boy.' He grinned.

'Why don't you come to us? I'm sure Claire and Steven won't mind. And we always have our main Christmas meal in the evening in any case. A tradition from when Dad used to work on Christmas Day. Claire and I couldn't bear to stop it.'

There was a quiver in her voice and it was pretty obvious she was upset at the memory. He knew her parents' death had hit her pretty hard — which was understandable. At the time, most of the pupils at school had sympathised and imagined how they might have felt under similar circumstances. But she'd been a difficult person to know back then. She'd shaken off all offerings of support.

She seemed to be in a mood to talk just now, though. He took a deep breath; he knew his attempt to reach out might well be rebuffed, but it was a risk he needed to take if he was to get anywhere near her. In other words, it was a risk worth taking.

'He was the manager at the hotel, wasn't he?' Ryan asked, casting his mind back to what he knew of the family. They hadn't lived here long when the accident happened, but it had been a huge tragedy for the area. And everyone had worried about the two teenage daughters the couple had left behind.

'Yes, he was.'

Ryan glanced over and her brave smile nearly broke his heart. He hardly dared to breathe. He wanted to comfort her — to take her in his arms and hug her until the pain he could see in her expression had softened.

'And what did your mum do?'

'She worked part-time as a reception-ist at the hotel. But she always arranged to have Christmas Day off.'

'Didn't her colleagues have something to say about that?' He winced inwardly, guessing he maybe shouldn't have been so blunt.

He was relieved when she laughed.

'They might have had something to say about favouritism,' she admitted. 'But Mum always volunteered to work at Hogmanay instead. She was quite happy to sacrifice partying the New Year in so she could spend Christmas Day at home with me and Claire.'

They jogged a little further in silence. He was strangely honoured that she had spoken to him about her parents in this way. He hoped it meant that he was beginning to earn her trust at last.

'They both loved their jobs so much.' She was speaking almost to herself now, and the wobble in her voice was more pronounced.

Purely on instinct, he slowed to a stop and took her in his arms and let her sob softly against his chest.

'Coming back here has brought it all back,' she admitted, pulling slightly away so she could look up at him with her eyes still bright with tears. If the lighting had been stronger, he was sure her nose would be red. But she was still more beautiful than he'd ever seen her before. 'I always miss them, of course,' she continued. 'Even when I'm in Edinburgh. But Aberbrig has a lot of memories.'

'It's bound to,' he said as he pulled her closer against him.

He didn't like to see her so unhappy. And he knew it wasn't his place to say, but he couldn't help thinking that, if she'd stayed, she might have been able to work through her grief by now and learn to live with her unhappy teenage years. As her sister had done.

That wasn't for him to point out, though. It was something she had to discover for herself.

'So,' she said, pulling away from his embrace and looking up into his face. 'Will you join us for dinner on

Christmas night? Or will you not?'

He took his time and smiled softly down into her eyes.

'I'd be delighted.'

8

Merry Christmas

Vicky was ridiculously excited about Christmas in a way she hadn't been since she was a small child. She didn't examine too closely why that might be.

She agonised for ages over what to buy for Ryan as a gift, though. It wasn't as though they were girlfriend and boyfriend. Not properly. Yes, they'd been out on dates and yes they spent time together — but there was always the knowledge in the background that there was a time limit to their relationship. As soon as Steven was better, she would be going back to her real life.

She kept having to remind herself of that because, around Ryan, it was very easy to forget.

There was no doubting, whatever

else was going on, that Ryan had quickly become her dearest and most trusted friend. And she wanted to get him a gift that would reflect that.

Claire's eyes narrowed as they discussed it before Vicky went to work.

'What do you mean by 'special present'? If you're too extravagant you might give him the idea that you're more serious about him than you're admitting.'

'No, he won't think that. Ryan knows how things are. He knows I'm not planning to stay around here long term.'

Claire gave a loud sigh and started to butter a slice of toast.

'I do wish you'd reconsider.' She glanced across at Vicky. 'I was only half joking when I said a while back that I hoped you'd meet someone and stay around. Ryan's lovely and he seems to really like you. And I've really liked having my wee sister close by these past weeks.'

Vicky didn't answer immediately.

Instead, she took her cup and plate over to the sink and quickly washed them, using the moments when she had her back to Claire to think about her reply.

'I've enjoyed being here,' she said at last. 'As far as I can. And you know I love you and Steven very much. But you also know how unhappy I was living in Aberbrig.'

'You didn't give the place a chance,' Claire accused. 'You'd made up your mind you weren't going to fit in and it became a self-fulfilling prophecy. And when we lost Mum and Dad you blamed Aberbrig for that, too.'

'That's not true. I was looking forward to our new life here.'

Claire gave a tiny shake of her head.

'You've attached all your negative feelings onto the place, instead of addressing the fact that even before the accident, you weren't settling in. But things could be different now. You're older. You've already made friends such as Ryan and Paula.'

Vicky sighed. She loved her sister

dearly, but Claire's attempts at amateur psychology left a lot to be desired. She'd overcome her fear of the place, but the truth of the situation wasn't any deeper than that Vicky was happier living elsewhere. Anywhere that wasn't Aberbrig.

She bit her lip. She really didn't want to talk about this. Not now, at least, not when the only purpose it would serve would be to upset everyone. And she was determined not to be upset this morning — not when she was thinking happy thoughts about spending some time with Ryan at Christmas.

'So, what do you think I should get him as a gift?' she said, swiftly changing the subject back to one she did want to discuss.

Claire shrugged.

'I don't know. Socks? A CD? A scarf?'

She was obviously not going to get any help from her sister, so she smiled sweetly and headed for the door.

'I've got a couple of hours owing, so I'll be back by three,' she said as she buttoned her coat over her uniform and slung her handbag over her shoulder.

'Good. I told Jack I'd try to check in at the office today. I know Steven's a lot better, but I'd still rather not leave him on his own.'

She nodded. Her brother-in-law had come a long way in a short time. Everyone was impressed with his recovery. But he had a tendency to push himself too far — as he had the day he'd ended up falling and she'd had to call Ryan to help. So it was as well not to leave him unsupervised too long because there were no guarantees he wouldn't try the same trick again now he was feeling stronger.

Her morning clinic was busy, so she didn't get a minute to worry about her gift-buying dilemma.

Though Joyce Imrie was in to have her ears syringed and seemed intent on discussing Vicky's supposed love life. Vicky was quick with her denial. But Joyce was having none of it.

'What do you mean you're not going

out with Ryan McGregor?' she asked with narrowed eyes. 'He's even taken you home to meet his mother. Of course you're going out with him.'

'How did you know he took me home to meet his family?'

'This is Kinbrae,' Joyce supplied with a knowing look. 'Everyone knows everything.'

Fair enough. Vicky had heard as much about the place.

Her romantic life was a private matter, though and Vicky smiled, intent on not discussing hers and Ryan's relationship with a patient. But Joyce wasn't an ordinary patient. She was a woman on a mission to discover the truth.

'Why on earth would he take you home to meet his family if you aren't going out?'

Vicky realised how silly the truth would sound — nobody around here was going to buy the 'just good friends' label. To all intents and purposes, it must look to everyone as though she

131

and Ryan were involved. Denial wasn't going to work — even if everyone was reading too much into the situation.

'I really can't imagine,' Vicky told her. And smiled again.

In truth, if circumstances had been different and she'd intended to stay around forever, she'd have loved to be Ryan's girlfriend. What woman wouldn't? He was gorgeous and lovely.

After her patient had left, Vicky tidied the treatment room. Then she left the surgery and walked the short distance from the surgery to McGregor's Café for her lunch.

'Hi there,' she called over to Paula, who was behind the counter — and she received a warm, welcoming smile.

She saw him as soon as she turned to look for a table; he was unmistakeable with that red hair. He was sitting in the far corner, looking at the menu. He seemed to sense her gaze and he looked up and smiled.

'I wasn't expecting to see you here,' she said as she approached.

He got to his feet and swooped down to brush his lips against her cheek — his kiss warmed her frozen skin and she smiled at him.

'I don't know,' she heard Joyce's voice say from a nearby table. 'You smile at him like that and still have the cheek to try to get me to believe you two aren't going out.'

Vicky ignored Joyce — and Joyce's voice — and continued to smile at Ryan.

'I thought I'd see if you wanted some company for lunch,' he said.

'Of course I'd like some company. This is a lovely surprise.'

He reached over and pulled out a chair for her and they both sat down.

'So,' she said. 'What are you really doing here?'

He sat back and looked at her closely, his blue eyes darkened to almost navy. He seemed to be weighing something up.

'I found I couldn't wait until our run tomorrow to see you again.'

Her breath caught as she considered

the implications of those words. Excitement vied with terror. She daren't let herself get too close to him. She daren't allow herself to love him — not when she was making plans to leave as soon as her sister no longer needed her. But she was powerless to stop the joy that made her heart leap.

'Ryan . . . I . . . '

He held up his hand.

'I know,' he said then his nose wrinkled. 'Too much.'

But he reached out and covered her hand with his, just the same. And his touch was warm and made her feel she belonged.

*　★　★*

As he made his way home after his Christmas Day shift, he reflected on recent events. It was only when Vicky had asked why he'd bothered to drive to Kinbrae on a busy afternoon, just to spend a lunch hour with her, that he'd realised: despite his best intentions, he was hopelessly, helplessly in love with her.

He shook his head. It was ludicrous that he'd fallen in love with a girl who had told him quite clearly that she didn't want to hang around long enough to form any kind of romantic relationship. But there it was — it had happened.

And the very odd thing was that he wouldn't have it any other way.

Now he had to work out how not to tell her. Because he knew it was something she didn't want to hear.

Vicky was everything he'd ever dreamed a woman could be: she was sweet and kind and incredibly beautiful. But there was more to it than that. There was something about her — an indefinable quality that made her special and made him realise without a doubt that she was the one for him.

'How was your shift?' Faye asked as he arrived home to change before going to see Vicky.

'Busy,' he answered. 'But not too

bad, considering. How's your day been?'

'Good,' she said with a smile. 'Tanya's mum cooked an enormous lunch and we all ate way too much. I've only popped home to fetch their pressies — I forgot to take them over. I'll probably stay over there tonight. I take it you're going to see Vicky?'

He grinned his reply.

Normally he would have been dead on his feet after all the minor injuries and emergencies he'd dealt with today, but knowing he was going to see Vicky gave him a second wind.

He tore off his scrubs and showered, before changing into a casual top and jeans. He grabbed Vicky's gift and the chocolate and wine he'd bought for Claire and Steven. Then he rushed around to see her.

She answered the door wearing a pretty red dress and a smile that made his heart beat faster. 'Hello,' she said. 'Come in out of the cold.'

'It's more damp than cold,' he said, before realising he sounded like an idiot; if she wanted a weather report she could listen to the radio.

He followed her into the hall, then reached out and took her arm with the hand that wasn't holding the bags with the gifts. 'Can we just have a minute before we join the others?'

She looked up at him expectantly.

'What's the matter?'

'Nothing's the matter.' He popped the bags onto the hall table, so he was free to take her in both his arms. She leaned against him with a sigh and he'd truly never felt happier. 'It's good to see you,' he told her, before his head descended towards her and he kissed her thoroughly.

She tasted of vanilla and spices and sweetness.

And he wanted the kiss to last forever.

★ ★ ★

Vicky knew, on a sensible level, that this wasn't a good idea. But kissing Ryan felt so good that she couldn't stop herself. And she justified the kissing by telling herself it was Christmas.

'We should join the others,' she said at last, still enclosed in his arms — his head bent so his forehead rested on hers. 'They'll be wondering where we are.'

'In a minute,' he replied. 'I want to give you your present, first.'

He picked up the smaller of the two gift bags and handed it to her, and she could feel him watching her carefully as she took it from him and peered inside. She fished out the small, gift-wrapped parcel and untied the red ribbon before tearing off the matching shiny paper. When she opened the box she gasped.

'Ryan,' she said as she gently touched the brilliant blue stone that hung from a gold chain.

'I thought of you as soon as I saw it,' he told her. 'The stone is the exact colour of your eyes.'

She was touched, but she was also uneasy.

'It's lovely. But I can't take it. It's too much.'

His face fell and she felt terrible. She didn't want to hurt him, but accepting such a personal gift would make things awkward.

'I thought you'd like it,' he told her quietly.

'I do like it,' she rushed to reassure him. 'I love it. But this is the kind of thing you'd buy for a girlfriend, not for a friend.'

'It might be the kind of thing a man would buy his best friend,' he said. 'If that friend happened to be a girl.'

Vicky wasn't convinced. But then she remembered how she'd spoken to Claire only a few days ago, about her need to find the perfect gift for Ryan — and then she understood.

'I didn't buy you anything this expensive,' she told him, biting her lip with sudden embarrassment.

Reaching for the locket, he smiled and her heart flipped over.

'Let me help you put it on,' he said,

and the need to argue abated.

There was no way she could refuse this lovely, thoughtful gift, so she turned around and lifted her hair out of the way. His fingers tickled at the nape of her neck as he fastened the chain. And, when his lips brushed the same spot in the lightest of kisses, she knew that the feelings they stirred up had nothing to do with friendship and everything to do with falling in love.

'I have your present here,' she said, reaching into a bag that was on the stairs and trying her hardest to ignore the realisation. 'I'm almost embarrassed to give you it after seeing what you've bought me.'

'Don't be silly, Vicky. You didn't need to get me anything, but I'm sure this is perfect.'

He ripped the paper off and took out the old-fashioned alarm clock she'd bought him.

'Sorry, it's lame.' She grimaced. 'I didn't know what to get you — then I remembered you said you had trouble dropping off and waking up when you were on night shift . . . ' She shrugged. 'I thought it would be useful.'

He enveloped her in a massive bear hug and kissed the top of her head.

'I love it, thank you.' And he sounded like he meant it so she smiled up at him.

'We'd best go and join the others. Dinner's nearly ready and they'll be wondering where we are.'

The Christmas meal was a lovely one. They had to eat at the kitchen table as the dining room was still being used as a bedroom. Steven was getting better by the day, but was still finding it difficult to negotiate the stairs. Kitchen or not, though, the turkey was cooked to perfection as were all the trimmings. They pulled crackers and laughed at the daft jokes and wore their hats until they fell down over their eyes.

Then they took their coffees through to the living room and played board games, laughing and joking noisily as they did so.

'This has been lovely,' Ryan said when it was getting late, 'but I'd better head off.'

Vicky saw him out.

'Thanks again for my present,' she told him on the doorstep, her hand involuntarily moving up to touch the stone.

'And thank you for mine.' He kissed her again and then he was gone and she was left staring down the street after him.

The necklace really was too much for a friend, she should feel highly uncomfortable. But, as she saw her reflection in the hall mirror, she could see Ryan had been right — the stone did match her eyes.

Knowing he'd been so thoughtful made her smile as she went to help Claire tidy up before bed.

★   ★   ★

'I think my sister has a man friend,' Joyce Imrie confided in Vicky when her clinic opened on the day after Boxing Day.

Vicky immediately felt sorry for Alice Imrie — it would be impossible to develop a romance with any degree of privacy when Joyce was your sister.

'That must be nice for her,' Vicky said mildly, keen not to encourage Joyce to gossip about her sister.

Joyce grimaced.

'She only moved back to Kinbrae recently. I should have known there was more to it than wanting to live near me.' Joyce harrumphed and Vicky felt immediately sorry for her instead.

'I'm sure she wants to be near you — even if she has met someone. The fact that you're her sister won't have changed. Now, can you take off your coat and roll up your sleeve, please, so I can take your blood pressure?'

As Vicky fastened the cuff around Joyce Imrie's upper arm, she listened as the older woman recited a list of complaints against her twin sister: Alice had cancelled their planned shopping trip twice in a row on a flimsy excuse; there had been meals missed; new clothes bought.

'And she's started using perfume,' Joyce supplied.

'Well, those things in themselves don't mean she's met a man,' Vicky told her reasonably.

'You're forgetting, we're very close — twins. I've always had an instinct about what might be going on in her life — even when she lived away from Kinbrae. And I've always been right.'

'Even if you are right about this, there's no reason it has to be bad news. If Alice has met someone and is happy, that would be good news, surely?'

'I've gotten used to having her around again,' Joyce confided a little forlornly. 'I don't want to lose her.'

'You won't,' Vicky said, quite certain about that. She didn't know either of the sisters well, but from what she did know, Alice was equally fond of Joyce.

'And I don't want her to be hurt,' Joyce got to the heart of the matter.

'She was engaged when we were younger. But the man in question broke it off and broke her heart in the process.'

'Not all men are alike,' Vicky said, thinking of Ryan — who was like no other man she'd ever met.

'You don't understand,' Joyce said quietly. 'I think the man she's taken up with is her ex-fiancé.'

Ah. Vicky could see at once why Joyce was so worried.

'Things might work out this time,' Vicky told her reasonably.

'But there's also a very good chance they won't.'

Vicky reached out and patted the other woman's arm. 'Alice is a grown woman,' she told her quietly. 'You wouldn't like if she took it into her head to tell you how to live your life, would you?'

'Indeed I wouldn't.'

'So Alice has to be allowed to make her own mistakes, even if she is repeating one from years ago. And searching for happiness and making mistakes in the process is a part of being human.'

Joyce nodded.

'I know. But I needed to talk to someone. And you have a sympathetic way about you.'

Vicky smiled. Joyce wasn't the first patient to have told her that — and she liked that people trusted her enough to confide their troubles in her. And she felt especially privileged that this normally sharp-tongued woman had taken to her.

Things were really going well for her at this surgery. A twinge of regret that she'd soon be leaving made her want to sigh. Instead, she smiled at her patient.

'Now, I need you to be quiet and still for a few minutes, please, so we can get the blood pressure measured.'

Joyce sighed, but sat back in her chair and let her arm relax onto Vicky's desk as the cuff inflated.

Vicky couldn't help thinking that it

might be an idea to suggest Joyce speak to her sister about the concerns she'd voiced this morning. When she'd recorded the readings she'd do just that.

9

Happy New Year

The days between Christmas and the New Year passed quickly and Steven seemed to be getting stronger with each hour. But then, on New Year's Eve — as Vicky was thinking of getting ready for the party at the McGregors' farm in Kinbrae — Claire had news.

'Steven and I won't be going tonight,' she said.

'Is there something wrong?' Vicky hadn't noticed anything amiss, but it wasn't like the couple to refuse an invitation to a party.

'Not as such,' Claire said. 'But Steven's been tired the past few days. I guess mending bones is taking a lot out of him.'

'I'll phone Ryan,' Vicky said immediately. 'Tell him not to bother dropping by to collect us.'

'No, you must go,' Claire insisted. 'Nobody expects you to stay home.'

'But I'm a nurse — what if you need me?'

Claire smiled.

'Steven will be fine,' she insisted. 'We'll have a quiet night in front of the TV, just the two of us. Like the first New Year's Eve after we married.' She smiled fondly at the memory. 'And, if we do need medical help, I'm perfectly capable of calling NHS 24.'

'But . . . '

'No,' Claire insisted. 'I won't hear of you missing this party. We appreciate everything you've done for us. I honestly couldn't have managed without you, but you have to lead your own life, too. Go out — have fun. And make sure you kiss Ryan at midnight.'

Vicky flirted briefly with the idea of arguing, but she knew Claire was right. She and Steven would be fine without her tonight. And she was glad about that as she was really, really looking forward to seeing Ryan. And to kissing him when the bells welcomed in the New Year.

★ ★ ★

Ryan had put the thought of Vicky leaving the area to the back of his mind. Now, though, he knew he'd have to face the issue; Steven was getting stronger by the day. And he knew she still had her room at the flat in Edinburgh. It was only a matter of time before she told him she was going.

When that happened they would have to talk. There were ways around geographical differences — especially these days with video chats and fast trains. He knew he couldn't let her go. She meant too much to him.

He parked the car outside her sister's house and smiled and waved as a noisy group of revellers called 'Happy New Year' in his direction.

Vicky had opened the door by the

time he was through the gate and she looked stunning in an ankle-length black dress with heels so high he was surprised she was able to stand in them, let alone walk. Her hair was up, exposing the curve of her neck and he breathed in her perfume as he bent his head to kiss her.

She rested her hands on his chest and smiled up at him. Even through the thick material of his jacket, her touch felt warm.

And he couldn't help noticing the pendant he'd given her for Christmas around her neck, the jewel nestled against her pale skin at the neckline of her dress. He was thrilled she'd liked his present enough to wear it when she was dressed up to go out.

'Hi,' she said. 'I'm afraid there's been a change of plan.'

He wasn't prepared for the disappointment that surged through him.

'Are you cancelling on me?' he asked in a half-jokey manner, not wanting her to know how upset he was by that idea.

She quickly shook her head and the feeling of relief was overwhelming.

'No, but Claire and Steven aren't going to make it.'

'What's wrong?'

'Steven's tired and they've decided it would be better if they had a quiet night in to greet the New Year.'

If his parents hadn't been expecting them, he'd have suggested they go back to his house and do the same. His housemates were out — and the thought of spending a quiet New Year's Eve in with Vicky was very tempting.

But his parents and a houseful of guests were waiting. It was doubtful that Mark would turn up, so their parents wouldn't be happy if a second son bowed out. Especially at such short notice.

And, while Mark was given special dispensation — being the quiet, artistic one meant everyone knew he was happier on his own than around crowds — his mother would be hurt if Ryan cancelled plans now.

Besides, Vicky looked stunning and he quite fancied showing her off.

'I'll get my coat.' She stepped away and he stood on the doorstep as she nipped back into the hallway.

There was no way he could let her end things between them. If he had been so worried by the thought she might be cancelling their date tonight, the idea he might never see her again filled him with dread.

'I'm looking forward to tonight,' she said, once they were on their way.

The road was icy and, despite the fact his car was a four wheel drive, he needed to keep all his concentration on getting them safely to Kinbrae, so he had to resist the urge to glance across. But he could hear the smile in her voice.

She could be happy here, if she let herself be. He knew it. She had a job she loved. She'd made friends. And she had a boyfriend who loved her more than anything. But it was obvious to anyone that the shadows from the past still wielded a mighty force over her.

He'd have to speak to her tonight — to try to convince her to stay. If he could convince her that he could make her as happy as she made him, then he knew she'd want to hang around.

'It should be a good party,' he replied to her comment. 'Mum always puts on a great buffet. And we generally get a good crowd.'

* * *

Vicky could well believe that to be true. Jack and Mark had been older and she hadn't really known much about them when she'd been at school. But she'd always known how popular Ryan was. And, since taking up her post at the surgery in Kinbrae, she had quickly come to realise that the entire family was highly regarded locally.

Nobody had a bad word for Heather and Denny McGregor, or their sons. Even the notoriously grumpy Joyce Imrie had only good things to say where they were concerned.

With that amount of goodwill towards them — and the general high spirits found in these parts at the New Year — their party was bound to be a success.

And, judging by the cars parked all the way up the lane to the farmhouse, everyone agreed that the place to be this New Year's Eve was at the McGregors' farmhouse.

'Sorry we have to park so far away from the house.' He cast her an apologetic smile.

'No worries.' Though, she did wonder about the wisdom of having borrowed her sister's highest heels: there were lamps lighting the way, but the ground running up to the house wasn't particularly even. And she still wasn't particularly steady on her feet in high shoes. But she always felt too small next to Ryan and had felt she needed the extra inches.

As though reading her mind, Ryan slipped his hand into hers and gave her fingers a reassuring squeeze.

'Best hold on in case I trip over,' he joked. And she was grateful for the safety net his touch provided.

They heard another vehicle pull up and they turned to find a McGregor's delivery van pulling up behind Ryan's car.

'Hello, you two.' Chrissy grinned as she got out of the van.

'Hello,' Vicky replied, genuinely pleased to see the other woman. 'Seems we arrived too late to get a good parking space.'

'I should have been here ages ago,' Chrissy confessed. 'I was supposed to be helping Heather to get everything ready. But I got held up on a delivery. I haven't even had time to get changed.' She grimaced down at her outfit, which Vicky could clearly see in the light from the lamps.

'You look lovely,' Vicky told her truthfully. It would be impossible for Chrissy to look anything else; even still dressed in her work jeans and jacket, her thick mane of bright auburn hair, clear skin and deep brown eyes stood out.

Then Vicky wished she hadn't said anything when Chrissy looked embarrassed.

'Come on,' Chrissy told them, recovering quickly. 'Let's hurry. It's freezing out here and we're missing all the fun.'

They walked up to the house together.

'Sounds like it's going well,' Ryan said as they got closer and the music and laughter reached them.

They wasted no time in joining the revellers who had set up a makeshift dance floor by pushing all the living room furniture back against the walls.

As Ryan took Vicky's hand and they stepped towards the centre of the room, the music changed to a slow number

'Did I tell you how beautiful you look this evening?' he whispered in her ear as he drew her close.

She giggled.

'Is that the drink going to your head?'

'I haven't had a drink.' He smiled. 'I'm stone cold sober. I'm driving,' he reminded her.

And she nestled a little closer because, at that moment in his arms, she believed him and she did feel beautiful.

They danced until her feet hurt.

'Do you mind if we sit this one out?' she asked.

Heather was over in an instant.

'Ryan, I've a batch of hot snacks just about ready. Can you come and help bring them out?'

'Can I help?' Vicky asked.

'No, it's fine,' Heather assured her and cast a smiling look down at Vicky's shoes. 'You rest your feet because I'm sure my son will have you dancing again before long.'

As soon as Ryan was gone, Paula took his seat.

'How are wedding plans going?' Vicky asked. The two had become friends over the time Vicky had been popping into the café. But it was difficult to talk for more than a few minutes at a time because Paula was always busy serving other customers between their exchanges.

'Very well, thanks,' Paula replied with a smile and Vicky couldn't help noticing how the other woman glanced across at her fiancé.

Vicky suppressed a sigh. Romance seemed so easy for other people — she'd never know why it was so difficult for her.

'You'll come to the wedding, won't you?' Paula asked.

Vicky hadn't been expecting that.

'Oh, you don't need to invite me,' she replied, appalled that Paula might think she'd been hinting that she wanted to go.

'I think I do.' Paula laughed as she patted Vicky's arm. 'Do you honestly think Ryan would forgive me if I didn't? Besides, the invitations went out ages before you arrived, otherwise you'd have been on the guest list from the start.'

Vicky's face grew warm as she smiled. Being included in this important event showed she was being accepted — that Paula saw her as more than just another customer. And she was thrilled.

'That's so kind,' she said, trying not to make a fool of herself by bursting into tears on the spot.

It was ridiculous: she wasn't planning on staying around for long, so it shouldn't matter to her that people liked her. But it did.

'Good. Glad that's settled.' Paula got to her feet as Ryan arrived back. 'I'm off to see if I can persuade my fiancé on to the dance floor,' she said and gave a little wave as she wandered off.

Vicky wasted no time in following Paula's example and she suggested to Ryan that they dance again.

'I thought your feet hurt.'

'That's easily remedied.' She kicked off her borrowed high heels then stood

160

up and reached out to him. Laughing, he took her hand and let her pull him to his feet.

Standing next to him in bare feet she felt tiny. He was so overwhelmingly tall, but she felt safe in his arms as they danced.

Ryan had gone to fetch cool drinks for them both when Joyce Imrie came up to her and sat beside her.

'Hello,' Vicky smiled, genuinely pleased to see the older woman. 'I didn't expect to see you here tonight.'

'I wouldn't have come,' Joyce admitted. 'But Alice was keen.' She nodded towards an older dancing couple and grimaced. 'Of course, I hadn't realised it was because she knew lover boy would be here.'

'They do look like they make a lovely couple,' Vicky offered reluctantly, not wanting to upset Joyce, but equally wanting to be positive about anyone who had found romance.

Joyce glanced over towards her sister. 'They do, don't they.' In that instant,

Vicky could see on Joyce's face all the worry she felt for her sister — and for herself.

'Things will work out,' she offered. She knew the words were clichéd and sounded empty, but she also knew what she said to be true. 'No matter how bad it seems now, one way or another it will all sort itself out.'

She only wished she could listen to her own advice. Because, as things stood, whenever she thought about the future, a tight knot twisted in her stomach.

Making a supreme effort to ignore the knot now, she smiled up at Ryan as he arrived back and handed Vicky her drink.

'Thank you,' she told him before taking a sip.

'Can I fetch you something?' he asked Joyce and the older woman shook her head.

'That's kind of you, Ryan, but I'll let you two get on with having fun.' She seemed about to walk away, but at the last moment she turned to Ryan. 'You've got a gem here,' she told him, nodding towards Vicky. 'You'd be an idiot to let her go.'

In her horror-stricken state, Vicky felt Ryan squirm at her side. And she sighed softly — not knowing whether to be relieved or hurt that he obviously felt the same way she did: a permanent relationship wasn't on his agenda.

Joyce walked away before Ryan could reply. And Vicky really didn't want to have the conversation here at this party, so she grabbed his arm and pulled him to the middle of the floor, determined to enjoy being with him as long as she could. Before long, they were dancing again and the moment was gone.

She couldn't believe how quickly the time flew. In the past, when she'd been to Hogmanay parties, the hours between arriving and the bells had seemed to last an eternity. But not tonight.

It could only be the company, she decided, flashing Ryan a wide grin.

With him, everything was fun.

As they approached midnight, Denny held up his hand to call for quiet and a hush fell over the party. Heather turned the radio on so they could all join in with the countdown.

And then everyone was calling 'Happy New Year,' and there was much hugging and kissing.

It was natural that Vicky put her arms around Ryan's neck and lifted her face for the first kiss of the New Year. And he seemed more than happy to oblige.

If anyone noticed that Ryan's lips lingered on hers longer than was strictly traditional for a New Year kiss, then they had the good manners not to mention it.

'I really enjoyed tonight,' she said as they made their way out to the car. It was freezing cold and, despite her coat, she shivered.

'Good,' he said, drawing her in towards the warmth of his body. 'Because I did, too.'

And, when he kissed her again, she

truly felt happier than she'd ever done.

Although that worried her. She shouldn't be getting too comfortable about her relationship with Ryan. She'd already given Joyce Imrie — and possibly half the village — the idea that she and Ryan were an item.

But her life was no longer in Aberbrig — nor in Kinbrae. Her life was miles away, in Edinburgh.

She didn't want to examine too closely why the thought of going back to that life made her feel so bleak.

10

Getting Serious

If it hadn't been for the other guests at the party, Ryan would have taken the opening Joyce had handed him and run with it.

He would have told Vicky that he never wanted to let her go.

As it was, he'd had to bite his tongue until he got her alone. And you couldn't get more alone than in a car in the early hours of a brand new year.

But how could he begin?

As he struggled to find the words, he noticed specks of white falling into the beams of the headlamps.

'It's snowing,' Vicky said and he could hear the excitement in her voice.

'You won't be so pleased if it settles and you have to drive this road to work.'

'Don't be such a misery,' she said,

but she was laughing and he couldn't help joining in.

That was what he liked most about Vicky — that she could make him laugh at a time when he would normally have been concerned that the snow was getting heavier by the second. A snowfall was never good news when you worked in A&E.

'This will be something and nothing,' she said gently, picking up on his thoughts. 'I'm sure it's just a flurry.'

They drove on in silence for a little while, but then he couldn't stand it any longer.

'About what Joyce said earlier.' His voice was strange — strained, not quite like him.

'It's OK,' she said. 'I saw your face, you don't need to say anything.'

'What did my face say?'

'Exactly what I was feeling — exasperation that Joyce won't stop singing that particular tune.' Her sigh filled the darkness of the car and the sound made his heart squeeze so tight he nearly gasped out loud. 'We both know this has to end.'

She'd got it wrong. That was not how he felt at all. But he couldn't find the words to tell her.

'My friends, my home, the place where I see my career developing, are all a long way from where you live your life,' she told him. 'And long-distance relationships don't work. At least not for me.'

He glanced across, but he couldn't see her features in the dark.

Someone had hurt her.

'Who was he?'

He felt a tiny movement that might have been a shrug. 'A doctor I went out with when I was a student. He went abroad to work and promised it would last. But of course it didn't. He met someone else.'

There was no bitterness in her tone, which suggested she was long since over that particular experience. But it had obviously made her wary. Unwilling to risk her heart again.

So, how could he tell her he loved her? When she'd just made it clear — again — that his confession would not be welcome?

'I'm sorry.' He didn't know what else to say.

There was that tiny movement at his side again.

'It's OK. It's all for the best. I wasn't as upset as I should have been, which made me think I didn't love him quite as much as I should have.'

'Well, that's OK, then,' he said, gripping the steering wheel so tightly that his knuckles hurt.

'But . . . ' She sighed again. 'I couldn't risk it happening with someone I knew I really cared about.'

She didn't say it. But he knew she was talking about him.

★ ★ ★

Even though the road back to Aberbrig was so dark that she couldn't see his expression, she knew there was

169

something wrong with Ryan. She could feel it with a certainty that seeped through to her bones. And it was pretty easy to work out what that might be, because he'd been quiet ever since they'd discussed Joyce's comment.

He was upset that people were reading more into their relationship than there was.

And it was understandable. He was young. He was gorgeous. He had a job he loved. The promise of his future lay out ahead of him like a blank page and he didn't want to be tied down by anyone's expectations or confined by their gossip.

'I'll speak to Joyce when I next see her,' she offered. 'I'll ask her not to spread any stories that aren't true. But please don't let a harmless comment upset you so much.'

His raking breath made her shudder.

'What if I told you that, for me, what she said rang true? That I don't want to let you go. Ever.'

Vicky's laugh filled the car, but the very fact he didn't laugh along with her told her all she wanted to know: he was deadly serious.

'Ryan . . . ' She didn't know what to say. Her heart leapt with joy that this lovely man would care so much for her. But her feelings from the old days paralysed her ability to move on. She could not live in Aberbrig. She'd never been happy there. And, even though she'd moved back to help her sister, she'd only managed because she'd known it was temporary.

They were in town now and arriving back in Claire's street. Ryan pulled into a space.

She could see his face now, in the light from the street lamps, and the bleak look on his face made her want to cry.

'Just think about it,' he asked. 'If you stayed, I'd spend every moment I could trying to make you happy — trying to make you forget the bad memories.'

She shook her head.

'Don't,' she pleaded. 'Please don't do this. We're having fun — that's all there is between the two of us. We agreed. And you didn't want anything long-term, either.'

There was silence. She held her breath.

His breath was released in one loud hiss.

'You're right,' he said. 'Put what I said down to the sentimentality of the season.'

She wasn't convinced.

'Ryan?'

'It's late. Let's get you back to the house.' He opened his door and the cool winter air rushed in. She shrugged and opened her own door to get out.

He walked with her to the steps and waited while she found the key in her bag and opened the door, but he made no attempt to touch her. She knew then that she'd ruined everything.

Why couldn't she be like other women? Anyone else would have been swept off their feet by Ryan telling them he wanted a serious relationship. Why did she have to be so hung up on past hurts?

'Hey, you two,' Claire greeted them in her dressing gown and slippers, with a smile on her face. 'Happy New Year.' She leaned forward to hug Vicky. Then did the same with Ryan.

'Happy New Year,' he told Claire brightly. But the smile didn't reach his eyes.

* * *

Ryan knew it was all his own fault. He'd ruined everything by wanting more than she was able to give. But he also knew that, given the time over, he'd have done exactly the same thing again.

He'd had no choice but to tell her how he felt about her. If he'd kept quiet, let her leave without saying a word, he'd never have forgiven himself. And, even while he knew her leaving was still some time away, he couldn't let himself fall any deeper for her without knowing she returned his feelings. Without knowing there was some chance she might change her mind and stay.

She phoned a little after midday and he was ridiculously pleased to hear from her.

'I'm glad we're OK,' she said. 'I was so worried I'd ruined everything last night.'

'You haven't ruined anything; it was all my fault,' he told her, quite happy to take the blame. 'As you said, we've both known since the start that we can't have a future together.'

'Let's not talk about that now,' she pleaded. 'I wondered if you were free for dinner tonight? Claire and Steven are going to see his parents and we'd have this place to ourselves.'

'I'm working,' he told her. 'There's a bug going around and a number of my colleagues are off sick, so I have to cover.'

'Oh.' She sounded genuinely disappointed and he didn't want to think about how her blue eyes would have darkened, or how her soft, cupid's bow pink lips would be pouting.

Best not to think of how she looked at all, really.

Even though the excuse was genuine, he was glad he was able to offer it — because he didn't think he'd be able to spend an evening alone with Vicky without making a fool of himself for a second night in a row.

★ ★ ★

Vicky had to reach the sad conclusion that Ryan seemed to be avoiding her. They'd decided not to run on New Year's Day, what with not getting home until the early hours. But he'd seemed relieved when he'd excused himself from dinner that night. And now, for two days in a row, he hadn't turned up for their morning run.

OK, so their running arrangement had been a casual one. And perhaps she should have phoned him to confirm

175

that he intended to go. But the truth was she was worried about calling him again after what had happened. She knew she'd upset him — she'd managed to upset herself, too — and speaking would be easier face to face.

If his face had turned up on the sea front for his morning jog, that was.

She drew cold air into her lungs, put her head down, and set off on her own for a second morning. This was going to be a short one she decided. Not only did she miss Ryan's company, but, if she was quick about her exercise, she might even have time for a warming bath before setting off. And maybe she could pop into Paula's when she got to Kinbrae, for some breakfast.

The thought of lovely treats ahead kept her feet moving.

Even if thoughts of Ryan constantly tried to disrupt her.

McGregor's was busy when Vicky arrived and she found a seat in the corner of the café. It was good to see the place so full. Paula had told her that it had taken the locals a while to accept a change of ownership. Seemed they were more than happy with arrangements now.

Paula was over in a moment to take her order.

'I think I'm going to have something sweet for breakfast,' she decided and Paula laughed.

'Why not?' she said. 'It's just the weather for it. Looks like it might snow today. And Heather's made some lovely Caramel Apple Betty. How about I warm up a piece of that for you?'

Vicky's mouth watered at the thought.

'Perfect,' she said. 'And some coffee, too, please.'

As she tucked into her breakfast, Joyce Imrie arrived and came over to the table.

'Do you mind?' she asked as she nodded to the empty chair. 'There don't seem to be many places free.'

Vicky reached over and pulled the chair out.

'It will be good to have company,' she

said, smiling at the other woman.

Joyce ordered a pot of tea and a slice of Victoria sponge.

'And make it a large slice, mind,' she called after Paula. 'If eating a large helping of something sweet is good enough for a nurse first thing in the morning, then who am I to argue?'

Vicky was momentarily horrified.

'Josh will be cross I'm leading his patients astray.'

Joyce threw back her head and laughed.

'My dear girl, I can assure you I was eating cake for breakfast before you were even born.'

And Vicky smiled.

'I'm glad I've seen you,' Joyce continued. 'I thought you'd like an update on the romance of the century.'

'Alice and her man-friend?'

'Alice and Trevor,' Joyce confirmed. 'They're official. Getting married. He's bought her a ring and everything.'

Part of Vicky was happy that Joyce's twin sister had, at last, got her happy ending with a man she obviously loved. But she was worried about Joyce, too.

'How do you feel about this development?' she asked cautiously, stirring her coffee so she didn't have to make eye contact and maybe intrude on any upset Joyce might be experiencing.

'Better than I was,' Joyce admitted happily and Vicky's head snapped up to see the other woman beaming broadly. 'I know I should have left well alone,' she said, 'but I spoke to him. I asked him straight out and it seemed he was as upset as Alice when they broke up last time and she moved away.'

'So you think it will last this time?'

'They have as good a chance as any other couple.'

'What about you? How do you feel about losing a sister to Trevor?'

'I've decided to look at it more like gaining a brother-in-law.' She smiled and attacked her cake with a fork. 'We're a small family — only the two of us left now. Trevor will mean there are three of us. And they plan to stay in

Kinbrae, so after years of my sister living a long bus ride away, I'll just have to take a hop, skip and a jump and I'll be in her parlour drinking tea.'

It all sounded good to Vicky.

And she couldn't help but see the parallels with her own life. What was left of her own family consisted of herself, Claire and Steven. And, even though the heartbreak that had precipitated her move from Aberbrig had been originated by losing their parents rather than a fiancé, she, too had run away from her feelings rather than face them.

She glanced at her watch and sighed.

'I'd best get going,' she told Joyce. 'I have a clinic starting soon.'

In reality, she didn't need to be at the surgery for another half an hour, but she knew that, as soon as she got in, there would be things to do: things that would stop her mind wandering too much.

It was only a short walk from the café to the surgery but the wind chill factor had Vicky looking in her pockets for her gloves. While distracted, she walked straight into someone.

The hairs on the back of her neck stood on end and she knew, without looking, who was there.

'Ryan.' His name was on her lips as their eyes met. He looked tired, as though he hadn't slept.

'I'm just off night shift,' he said. 'Still staff off sick and the rest of us are having to pick up the slack. I'm sorry I missed our run, but I'd hoped to catch you before you left for work.'

'I've just been for breakfast,' she explained, even though he hadn't asked.

'I know, Claire told me where I'd find you. Do you have a minute?'

She nodded, her plans for an earlier than necessary start forgotten.

'Can we walk?' he asked.

They stepped along the main street and towards the park. It would be quiet at this time in the morning, she hoped.

There were a couple of dog walkers way in the distance, but otherwise they had the place to themselves.

'I missed you,' she told him, then she could have bitten her tongue off. He didn't want to know that. He was weary from overwork. And, more importantly, she didn't want him reading any more into her comment than she meant.

He raked a hand through his red hair and grimaced.

'Did you.'

'Actually, yes. I hate running alone.'

He smiled, but didn't seem amused.

'We really need to talk, Vicky,' he told her quietly and her heart lurched.

This didn't look good.

If he asked her to stay she would be torn between what she wanted and what he wanted.

It was such a mess.

She longed for Ryan to take her in his arms, to kiss her, to tell her that everything would be OK. But how could it be when they wanted such different things? Besides, he didn't look like a man who was about to make a romantic move.

'What do you want to talk about?' she asked, not sure she wanted to hear.

'Us.'

The word hung in the cold morning air between them. And she certainly didn't want to discuss it. Because it could only go one way.

'We can't go on like this, Vicky,' he said, holding his hands out to her. 'I love you. I can't just be friends with you. And it kills me to know that all the time we're together you're planning to leave me.'

He loved her.

That was all that mattered. For a moment her heart soared.

And then it fell flat.

'I can't stay in Aberbrig, Ryan.' She paused, pleading silently for understanding. None was forthcoming. 'I just can't. I've told you how miserable I was, why I left. I told you from the start I was only here temporarily, while Claire needed me.'

He nodded once, but the action held no compassion.

'You can't ask me to carry on as we are,' he said.

She shook her head.

'I wouldn't.'

As they walked through the park, it started to snow. But Vicky couldn't get excited about it. Not even when the snowflakes grew thick and started to settle on the grass.

'Then what do you want to do?' He sounded weary.

She shrugged.

'I guess there's only one thing we can do.'

He nodded again. 'I guess I'll see you around, then.'

And, just like that, it was over.

He turned and walked away, his shoulders hunched up against the cold in his thick wool coat. And she let him go. Hardly daring to believe she could be so stupid.

She was letting Ryan McGregor go. *The* Ryan McGregor. The golden boy who had grown into such a man that she couldn't imagine ever meeting anyone else even half as wonderful.

But, more to the point, he'd told her he loved her and, though she'd been tempted, even that hadn't swayed her decision to leave. So it had to be the right choice for her.

Didn't it?

11

Snow Days

Ryan was too weary to even think of driving home to Aberbrig, so, when he got back to his car, he headed up to the farmhouse.

Heather McGregor always kept beds aired for her sons and for her granddaughter. Not that the sons used those beds often. But the thought of crawling under a duvet in his old bedroom had never been more appealing.

'Good morning, darling,' his mother greeted, immediately pouring him a cup of hot tea. 'Can I fetch you something to eat?'

'Maybe later,' he said. 'But I thought I'd go for a lie down, if that's OK. I've been on duty all night.'

If Heather McGregor wondered why

her youngest son wanted a lie down in his childhood home rather in the house he now lived in, she didn't ask.

Maybe she saw something in his face that stopped her curiosity in its tracks. Or maybe she realised he needed time. Whatever the reason, he was grateful for the fact his mother had always been a wise woman.

He passed out as soon as he pulled the cover over his weary body.

And he didn't dream.

Not even of Vicky.

But, as soon as he awoke, the horror of their morning conversation nearly overwhelmed him. He'd lost her. He'd even admitted, in the heat of the moment, that he loved her. And, instead of falling into his arms and telling him she loved him back — as he was sure she did — she'd retreated.

And it hurt like crazy.

He grabbed some clean clothes from his chest of drawers: jeans and a top that hadn't made it into the pile of clothes he'd taken with him when he moved out. Then he had a quick shower before going downstairs in search of food.

'Did you have a nice rest?' his mother asked.

'I did, thanks, Ma.' From somewhere, he managed to find a smile for his mother — even though he couldn't remember a time in his life before where he'd felt less like smiling.

He sat at the table to drink his tea and, without asking, his mother set a bowl of homemade vegetable soup and crusty bread in front of him.

'Thank you.' This time his smile was a little easier. Not that food was any substitute for Vicky, but at least if he was eating his attention would be diverted. Besides, his mother's vegetable soup had always been his favourite meal.

'I wondered whether or not to wake you,' Heather admitted, nodding towards the window. 'I wasn't sure about your shifts and I thought you might want to get home before things get any worse.'

He followed his mother's gaze and was surprised to see that, in the time he'd been dead to the world, outside had been transformed by a thick snowfall.

'How long was I asleep?' he asked at last. Though it couldn't have been that long as there were still the last rays of daylight lighting up the sky.

'It's gone three,' she said.

'I'll just finish this then I'll get out of your hair.' He picked up his spoon.

'You're very welcome to stay,' she told him.

'I know.'

But he'd rather be in his own home. Keeping this front of normality up in front of his family would be impossible long-term. He knew his housemates were at home, but Faye and the others didn't know him as well as his mum did. Disguising a broken heart would be much easier in front of his friends than it would in the company of his family.

Though, he did wonder at how good a job he'd done. His mother hadn't mentioned Vicky once, which made him think she'd realised something was up.

★ ★ ★

'Vicky, you'd better get away,' Josh told her as she tidied up after her last clinic.

She glanced towards the window.

'I'll just put these notes away, then I'll be on my way.'

He nodded.

'Just take it easy when you go. The roads between here and Aberbrig have been gritted, but it's been snowing heavily all day, so it will still be treacherous in places.'

'You don't need to worry,' she laughed. 'I appreciate your concern, but I'm a big girl and I've driven in snow loads of times.'

She wasn't quite as confident once out of the village. The snow had drifted and, in places, was almost as high as the car at the side of the road. She took things slowly, though, and made good progress. Until she reached the final hill a couple of miles away from home.

However hard she tried, her car would simply not reach the top. For every metre she drove forward, it seemed she slid two back. In the end, in despair, she slid into the side of the road and turned the engine off.

Exhausted from the amount of concentration she'd used to get this far, she leaned her head against the steering wheel for a few moments.

Taking a deep breath, she dug her mobile from her pocket. It was as she expected — the hills around here were notorious for having no signal.

Not that it would have been easy for anyone to rescue her, but at least she could have let her sister know she was OK.

She sighed.

At least she'd managed to drive most of the distance — that was something to be positive about. The rest of the way was walkable. And, luckily, Claire had popped a winter kit into the boot of her car. At the time, Vicky had accused her of fussing. Now, however, she realised she owed her sister a very big bunch of flowers. And, possibly, some chocolate.

She opened the boot and, ignoring the shovel as it would take more than that to get her over the crest of the hill, she took out the fleece, waterproof trousers and boots. As a final flourish, she wound the scarf around her head and neck and then popped the hat Claire had provided onto her head.

There! She was ready for an expedition to the North Pole, let alone a teeny stroll back to town.

Half an hour later, she realised she'd misjudged the distance. And the hills. As she trudged up the next snowy slope, she knew that, even had her car made it over the crest of the last one, this one would have defeated it.

And it wasn't even as though she could flag another vehicle down and ask for help. In all the time she'd been on the road, she hadn't seen another car. The roads around here were always quiet, but today they were eerily so. It seemed all the other commuters had considered the journey too risky.

She was considering going back to the car to sit it out when she heard it — the sound of a vehicle approaching. It sounded like it was coming from Kinbrae and headed for Aberbrig, but at this stage she would have begged a lift in either direction.

When it came into view though, her heart nearly stopped. It was Ryan's car.

*   *   *

Ryan had been looking out for Vicky since he'd spotted her abandoned blue Mini on the side of the road. His heart lurched now as he spotted the lone figure battling through the elements on her way home.

He could barely believe how far she'd

managed to walk. She must be exhausted.

He carefully stopped beside her, although he knew that probably wasn't wise. Stopping would lose the momentum he'd built up and it would be touch and go whether they'd make it to the top of this hill, even in his four-wheel drive.

He wound down the window.

'Vicky, get in. Quickly.'

She looked at him, her face pale and her eyes wide.

'Hi, Ryan.' Her smile was strained.

'Get in,' he said again. 'It's freezing.'

'I'm fine,' she said and, again, that forced smile was in evidence.

'You can't possibly walk all the way home.'

'I'm doing OK.'

She was just being stubborn now. He'd never seen Vicky like this before. Although her refusal to even consider staying on in Aberbrig had hinted at that trait.

While he'd had no choice but to give

in to her then, at the moment his priority was to get them both safely back to town. The snow was continuing its merry fall and very soon the entire road would be impassable.

'Vicky, I'm not going to argue with you. You need to get in now.'

Her eyes widened at his nurse-in-charge tone and he regretted at once that he'd been so firm. But it was for the good of both of them. He wouldn't leave without her. And it would be downright dangerous for them to spend the night out here.

She'd realise that in time and thank him for it.

Though she didn't look in the least grateful as she opened the passenger door and climbed in.

She brought the cold air in with her and he turned the heating up a little. He didn't want her being cold even if she had broken his heart.

'What were you still doing in Kinbrae?' she asked as he eased the car to the top of the incline.

'Went to see Mum.' He let out a sharp breath as the wheels spun and the car made little progress. 'I can't believe you would try to walk back to Aberbrig in this. What were you thinking?'

'My car doesn't cope well with snow and I needed to get home.'

'You should have stayed with the car,' he said quietly.

She didn't reply, but he could feel she was annoyed.

'I'm sorry,' he said, relieved as his own car made it to the top of the hill now. 'I just don't want anything bad happening to you. And walking home in this weather isn't the most sensible idea you've ever had.'

He glanced across and she smiled — and his heart cracked a little.

'My frozen feet would agree with you.' She grimaced. 'I just couldn't face the thought of spending the night in the car.'

'Just as well I happened along, then.'

'Yes,' she said quietly.

They didn't speak again until he

drove slowly into Claire's street. The journey had taken a good deal longer than it should have — at least three times as long. And the atmosphere had been strained.

'Nobody would have blamed you if you'd let me walk,' she told him as she undid her seatbelt.

'I'd never have done that.'

She smiled, then leaned across and kissed his cheek. Her lips were still cold and he longed to take her in his arms and warm them up with a proper kiss. But he knew that wouldn't have been appropriate.

Instead, he smiled back.

'I know you wouldn't,' she told him. 'And that's just one of the things that makes you a very lovely man.'

Before he could reply, she'd jumped from the car and was disappearing in through the front door.

And, even though it had been dark for a while, it felt to him as though the sun had just disappeared over the horizon. His world was going to be a much colder and darker place without her.

But he was going to have to find some way of coping.

⋆   ⋆   ⋆

Vicky woke up the next day to even more snow. Claire had said she'd drive her back to fetch her car when the roads had been cleared: that was obviously not a journey they'd be doing today.

As soon as she was dressed, she phoned Josh.

'I'm not going to make it in today, I'm afraid,' she told him apologetically and quickly explained the situation with her car and the amount of snow in Aberbrig.

'I wasn't expecting you,' he told her. 'None of us are going anywhere for the next wee while. I only hope the snow lets up long enough for the council to clear the roads.'

'I'm sure it will,' she said. Though she wasn't sure she believed it. It just seemed like the right thing to say.

'Well, until you are able to get in you're not to worry. There's a health visitor in the village — she normally works in Aberbrig, but she'll be as stuck as everyone else. She always helps out at times like these.'

Vicky was pleased that Josh had plans to cope and went to fetch a cup of coffee and some toast.

'Jack's keeping the office closed today.' Claire was waving her mobile when Vicky went into the kitchen. 'He's had to stay there overnight, but he doesn't want anyone else getting stuck.'

Vicky's eyes widened.

'He's staying at the office?'

'I offered to let him stay here,' Claire said. 'But he's quite happy on the sofa in his office. Says it means he can get more work done. So I've just got to help spread the word. Then I can join you in a lazy day.'

'Oh, no,' Vicky told her, appalled at the thought. 'I'm a trained nurse and I'm within walking distance of a surgery and a hospital. I have to help out. Staff won't be able to get in.'

Just as the health visitor who lived in Kinbrae was going to be covering for her, it was her duty to fill in for other stranded health workers. Especially when she knew there would be a huge number of patients looking for help with the aftermath of falls and the effects of winter vomiting and flu. Every nurse she knew would be making their way to the nearest hospital or surgery — even if it wasn't the one they were normally based at.

'I didn't think.' Claire bit her lip. 'Do you need to use the phone?'

'It's OK, I'll use my mobile.'

She phoned the local GP practice first and was grateful when they told her that they would appreciate her help.

That meant she wouldn't need to volunteer at the hospital, which would keep her safely out of Ryan's way.

She was professional enough to have gone wherever she was needed. But she couldn't pretend she wasn't grateful that she wouldn't have to run the risk of seeing him today.

It had been so awkward between them in the car that she knew he must feel the same way.

The surgery was much larger than the one in Kinbrae — which was understandable as Aberbrig was a much larger place.

'I'm Charlotte, one of the practice nurses — and I can't tell you how glad I am to see you.' Charlotte looked as though she might hug Vicky for having the good grace to turn up. 'There are normally three of us, but I'm here on my own today. One's off sick and the other couldn't make it in through the snow.'

Vicky smiled, pleased her offer of help was appreciated.

'I'll do my best to take some of the load off you. If you want to tell me what you need me to do, I'll make a start.'

'Fab — this way to the treatment room. There's an ear clinic due to start in five minutes. If you can run that it'll mean I can deal with the walking wounded from the ice rink that passes for a path outside. There have been a number in already, looking for sympathy and a bandage.'

The clinic was busy and Vicky was pleased when lunchtime arrived and they were able to take a quick break.

'Did you go to Aberbrig High?' Charlotte asked over coffee and a sandwich at lunchtime. 'Your face looks familiar.'

A cloud of impending doom settled on Vicky. She hadn't recognised Charlotte, but it seemed her unhappy school past was about to catch up with her.

'I did go there for a while,' she said.

'I knew it; I do know you,' Charlotte slammed a hand down on the staff room table. 'You didn't have the best of times at school, did you?'

Vicky smiled.

'You could say that.'

Charlotte reached out and patted her hand.

'We were on your side, you know. Everyone was so sorry when you lost your parents. But you seemed so self-sufficient and insular it was difficult to approach you.'

This was similar to the opinion Claire had shared with her recently and Vicky began to wonder if there was something in it. Yes, she had been miserable. Who wouldn't have been under the same circumstances? But could her unhappiness have radiated out and repelled possible friends?

'Maybe if we'd been older we'd have known how to help . . . '

'It wasn't your fault,' Vicky rushed to reassure. 'I didn't handle the move well in the first place. Losing our parents compounded issues.'

'How are things now?' Charlotte asked.

Vicky found herself nodding.

'Good, thank you. I seem to be happier in my own skin these days.'

'Well it's nice to meet the real you at last,' Charlotte said. 'And we mustn't lose touch. A crowd of us still get together for the odd night out. Perhaps you'd like to join us next time?'

'Yes, thank you. I'd love to,' Vicky said and she was startled to find she meant it.

And even more startled to realise that the lovely people she was meeting now had lived in Aberbrig all the time.

* * *

It had stopped snowing by early afternoon. And, over the following few days, the council were able to clear the roads sufficiently for people to go about their normal business.

'Ready?' Claire asked as she wound her scarf tightly around her neck and slipped on her coat.

'Absolutely,' Vicky answered and she picked up her bag.

Claire was taking her to pick up her car and then she was going to drive herself on to work in the surgery at Kinbrae from there. Much as she'd enjoyed working with Charlotte, she was looking forward to getting back to her own treatment room.

'There it is,' Vicky cried, pointing as the blue bodywork came into view.

Claire's eyes narrowed.

'Someone's cleared the snow off it,' she said. 'And it looks as though they've dug out the snow from under your wheels so you can drive onto the road.'

Her car had, indeed, been cleared — and her heart filled with gratitude for the person who had carried out this good deed. She and Claire had been prepared for a very cold hour with their spades.

'Who do you think did it?' Claire asked.

Vicky undid her seat belt.

'I don't know.' She shrugged. Though her mind was working overtime. 'The snow magician?'

'I don't think there's such a thing.' Claire laughed. 'I think it was Ryan. I don't know of anyone else who would have gone to the bother.'

If she was honest with herself, neither did Vicky. And her heart squeezed so hard she could barely breathe as she realised exactly what kind of man he was. And just how utterly stupid she was that she had allowed a chance of happiness with him to slip through her fingers.

But it was too late for all that now. She'd made her decision and even if she'd wanted to change her mind, things had been so awkward between them in the car the other day, it would be impossible to put them right.

It was all over.

12

Emergency

'Good to see you, Vicky,' Josh said with a smile. 'We've all missed you. Heaven knows how we're going to cope when you take off and abandon us completely.'

'I've missed all of you, too,' she said — and she really meant it. She'd had a lovely, if busy, time with Charlotte at Claire's local surgery, but coming back to Kinbrae was almost like arriving home. The familiar faces, the friendly waves and calls of 'hello' all lifted her spirits.

The first patient in her clinic was a familiar-looking redhead: Jessica McGregor — Jack's teenage daughter and Paula's soon-to-be step-daughter. Vicky knew her from the café as she often helped out there.

She smiled at the girl.

'School still off?'

'Yes — we're going back tomorrow. We had all hoped the snow would last a bit longer so the bus couldn't get through.' She grimaced and Vicky laughed. 'I've been staying with Gran because Dad got stuck in town. I'm hoping he'll be able to get home today, though.'

'I'm sure he will,' Vicky told her. 'The roads were quite clear when I came to work this morning.'

Jessica nodded.

'We thought as much when Uncle Ryan made it through first thing. Dad will probably give it a try when he's sorted things at the office. He gave the staff time off.'

'I know,' Vicky smiled, trying to ignore the way her heart had fluttered at the mention of Ryan's name. 'Remember, my sister Claire works for him? Now, how can I help you today, Jessica?'

'My ears have been popping,' Jessica

replied. 'And my hearing's not so good. I think it might be wax. I'd have asked Uncle Ryan to have a look, but he was in a rush when he arrived. He barely spoke to anyone. Then he grabbed a shovel and drove straight off again.'

So, Claire had been right — Ryan had been her snow magician. She would have to thank him because that had been incredibly kind under the circumstances.

As she examined Jessica's ears, they chatted about the forthcoming wedding. And Vicky knew she'd have to speak to Paula. When the invitation had been issued, Vicky had been seeing Ryan and it had been natural that she would be invited. Now, though, it was a different matter.

'I'm really looking forward to it,' Jessica told her now. 'My dress is off the shoulder and so pretty.'

'Off the shoulder?' Vicky glanced towards the window. 'Let's hope it warms up by then, or you'll freeze.'

Jessica laughed.

'We have shawls, too — just in case it's cold.'

Vicky knew all this from speaking to Paula and Claire, but she let the girl talk about her bridesmaid outfit.

'You're going to look gorgeous,' she told Jessica with a smile. 'Now, about these ears — have you been unwell at all over the past week? Have you had a cold? Or flu?'

'I had a bit of a sniffle,' Jessica confessed. 'But it wasn't anything much.'

Vicky nodded.

'I think the blocked sensation you're describing is as a result of that. It's nothing to worry about and it should clear up in the next few days.'

Jessica looked a little embarrassed.

'So I don't need to have my ears syringed.'

'No — not this time.' Vicky smiled reassuringly. 'But you absolutely did the right thing coming to see me. You can speak to me or to Dr Carter any time you're worried about anything.'

That earned her a grateful smile from Ryan's niece.

★ ★ ★

'What happened to you?' Faye exclaimed, obviously appalled at the look of Ryan as he came through the door, frozen and wet from melted snow.

He took off his soaked jacket and stamped his feet in an attempt to get his circulation going.

'I took a shovel to the snow around Vicky's car.'

There was silence for a moment, but he could see loud and clear by Faye's expression that she thought he was daft.

'Well,' she said at last. 'I hope she was pleased.'

He shrugged.

'She doesn't know. She wasn't there.'

'So, let me get this right in my head: you've just taken it upon yourself to randomly stop to dig her car out?'

'It wasn't random,' he said. 'It was

deliberate. I could hardly leave it for her to do.'

He shuddered as he thought of the tiny Vicky working for ages in the cold to do a job it had taken him the best part of an hour. The car had been in deep — not only covered by what had fallen from the sky, but also banked in by feet of snow that had been pushed to the side and impacted by the ploughs.

'After all she did to you I think leaving it for her to deal with is exactly what you should have done.'

'She didn't do anything,' he said quietly. 'She told me from the beginning that she wouldn't be staying in the area for long. I'm the one who changed the rules and wanted more.'

Faye shook her head.

'Go and get out of those wet clothes and into a nice warm bath. I'll have some soup heated up for you by the time you get back down.'

He grinned.

'Thanks, Faye — you're a pal.'

Vicky raised a hand in an uncertain wave at the couple who were walking carefully on the icy path on the opposite side of the street. She knew the McGregors were the nicest people in the world, but even nice people could be tetchy towards a woman who had hurt their son.

Heather McGregor's smile seemed genuine, though. But then her gaze fluttered back to her husband and Vicky could see, even from this distance, the expression of worry that crossed her face.

And now that Vicky looked at Denny McGregor, she could see he didn't look at all well: his complexion was an alarming red and purple. As she watched, he fell to his knees in the snow, clutching his left arm to his chest.

Heather's cry of distress reached her and Vicky raced across the road and knelt beside him.

'Denny, are you OK?'

213

'He's been ill for a couple of days.' Heather's distress was plain to see; it was obvious she was on the verge of tears. 'I've been on at him to call the doctor. That's why we're here — I was hoping to persuade him to see Josh.'

'What's wrong?' Vicky asked.

'He's been complaining of heartburn and chest pains and generally feeling unwell.'

'I'm fine,' Denny said breathlessly. 'Really. It's indigestion.' But his grimace told another story.

It didn't look good. To Vicky's trained eye, it seemed very likely Denny McGregor was having a heart attack.

Keeping as calm as she could, she turned to Heather.

'You need to phone 999 and ask for an ambulance,' she said. 'And then run across to the surgery and tell Josh he has to come immediately. And tell him we have a patient in cardiac arrest — he'll know what to bring.'

With a tiny gasp the only sign that,

beneath the surface, Heather was very nearly falling apart, she took her mobile out of her handbag and dialled.

'Tell them to hurry,' Vicky added as Denny slipped to the cold ground, unconscious.

Vicky quickly knelt beside him and melting ice and snow soaked through the thin trousers of her uniform.

'Denny,' she called. 'Can you hear me?' There was no response and Denny had stopped breathing, his complexion now pale.

She quickly checked his pulse and breathing.

Nothing.

Vicky was performing chest compressions on the patient when Josh arrived. They both continued to work on Denny McGregor until the paramedics came.

Before she got into the ambulance, Heather paused and put her hand on Vicky's arm.

'Thank you for what you did today,' she said, with a little break in her voice. 'I won't forget it.'

215

And then she climbed in and they were off towards the hospital with sirens blaring.

Once the vehicle rounded the bend from the main street and was out of sight, Vicky knew she had to make a call.

Still out on the street, the trousers of her uniform soaked and her legs frozen from where she'd knelt to treat Denny McGregor, she punched in Ryan's number.

He answered immediately.

'Vicky.'

'I don't want you to panic,' she told him, managing to keep her voice calm, even though she felt anything but. She'd dealt with patients in cardiac arrest before, but working on the father of someone who meant so much to her had been an entirely different matter.

'Vicky, you're scaring me, what's wrong?'

There was only one way to do this — and that was to say it straight out.

'Your father's been taken ill. He's on his way to hospital.'

She quickly gave him the details and wished she was doing it in person. She hated to think of him on his own when he heard this news. But she knew he'd want to be at the hospital when his parents arrived. His mother would need support — and she was sure he'd want to be close at hand to speak to the doctors about his father's condition.

The phone had been her only choice.

'Thank you for letting me know.' He sounded detached — cold even — and so unlike himself. But she knew that shock did strange things to people and the news she'd just given him would have upset anyone.

With a sigh, she replaced the phone in her pocket.

All she could do now was pray that Ryan's father would be OK and head off to her clinic.

★　★　★

When Vicky's name had popped up on his phone, he'd been elated. But his feelings had quickly turned to despair.

Knowing his father had been taken ill and that he hadn't been there to help was an odd feeling. And now he felt he was in some sort of parallel universe.

Vicky had assured him that his father had received help quickly and that was always a hopeful thing in these circumstances. But, even while he knew Vicky was a skilled and experienced nurse and that Josh was an excellent doctor, Ryan wouldn't be able to rest until he'd seen his father's condition for himself.

He phoned his brother Jack before he drove off. Jack promised he'd phone Mark and then meet Ryan at the hospital.

His father was still being seen by the doctors when he arrived.

'He's got a good chance,' he said, slipping his arm around his mother's shoulders. 'Vicky said she and Josh started treatment immediately.'

Heather McGregor nodded.

'Vicky was wonderful. I don't know what state your father would be in if she hadn't been there.'

Ryan was silent. He didn't want to say anything else when he didn't know the full facts yet. Best to wait now to see what the doctors said.

'I think we could use some coffee, Ma. What do you say?'

She nodded.

One cup of coffee later, and Jack arrived.

'How is he?' he asked as he ran an unsteady hand through his mane of red hair.

'We're waiting to hear,' Ryan said.

'You work here, don't you? Can't you go and find out?'

Ryan knew his brother's sharp tone was a result of being worried, but everyone else was worried, too. And, if he was honest, he'd been tempted to go and demand answers himself. But he'd also been on the other side of things and he'd experienced many times the nightmare scenario where worried family members got in the way of treatment.

'We have to let the doctors and nurses do their job,' Ryan said. 'Dad's in good hands. These are my colleagues and they know what they're doing. And we have to give the courtesy of letting them get on with it.'

Jack raked a hand through his hair again and sat down.

'You're right. I'm sorry.'

Ryan nodded in acknowledgement. Jack's apology was a first for him. His big brother always liked to be the one in charge — and he liked to be right. If the situation hadn't been so serious he might have relished this milestone for a moment. But, as it was, he was only pleased he'd managed to calm his brother down.

'Did you get hold of Mark?' their mother asked, still looking pale and strained.

'He'll be here as soon as he can,' Jack told her.

By the time Mark arrived, there was news:

'They think your father will pull though.' Heather McGregor hugged her middle son tight, tears of relief running down her cheeks.

Mark smiled broadly.

'That's good news,' he said.

They were allowed to see Denny shortly after that. And, even though he was still poorly and recovery would take some time, the faces around his bed were all smiles as they anticipated that recovery.

* * *

Had it been any other patient, Vicky would have gone to the hospital on her return to Aberbrig from Kinbrae, to see if there was news. So that's what she did with Denny McGregor. Even though she knew Ryan would be there and things might be awkward.

As it turned out, she ran into Ryan as soon as she arrived — in an almost exact replay from the day she'd turned up when Steven had been brought in.

'I'm sorry,' she said, stepping back.

She looked up uncertainly, trying to gauge his reaction.

'How is he?'

'It's good news,' he told her with a smile. 'He's stable and they're optimistic.'

She smiled back.

'That's great. And how's your mum doing?'

'OK,' he replied. 'Though I don't think it's hit her yet how close we came to losing him today. Mark's taken her home and he'll stay with her until Dad's discharged.'

It was good to hear him being so optimistic about the future.

'I know this probably isn't the time, but I need to thank you for clearing the snow from my car.'

'What makes you think it was me?'

For a moment, she wavered — what if it hadn't been him after all? Then she smiled.

'Jessica mentioned you'd stopped off at the farm to collect a shovel.'

He laughed.

'I should have known — Kinbrae gossip.' He shook his head in mock exasperation. 'I didn't expect my own niece to tell tales, though.'

'You can't do anything in Kinbrae without everyone knowing about it.' She smiled. 'Seriously, it was so kind of you. Especially with how things ended between us.'

A shadow crossed his face for a moment and she wished she hadn't mentioned the end of their relationship.

'You don't need to thank me for anything after what you did today. Mum's done nothing but sing your praises.'

'That's hardly the same.'

'No,' he agreed. 'No, it isn't. What you did can never be repaid.'

'It's what I'm trained to do,' she told him quietly. 'Any nurse would have done the same. You know that as well as I do.'

13

Wedding Bells

For a while, Vicky was the hero of the hour in Kinbrae. Her clinics had never been busier as everyone wanted to speak to her. She suspected at least half her patients had exaggerated their symptoms in order to get an appointment.

And she bore their curiosity with good grace — even if she was a little embarrassed by their praise. Because she realised it ultimately stemmed from their deep concern for Denny McGregor and from gratitude that he was recovering.

Over the weeks, though, things went back to normal. And only the hardened busybodies were still discussing the incident. And some of them also included a little regretful aside about

Vicky's imminent departure from Kinbrae.

'I really don't know why you have to move back to Edinburgh,' Joyce Imrie told her when she came in to get her blood pressure checked. 'You're useful to have around.'

She stifled a smile — this was praise indeed coming from the hyper-critical Miss Imrie.

'I'm sure Dr Carter wouldn't dream of employing a nurse who wasn't useful. My successor will, I'm sure, be equally handy.'

'It won't be the same,' she said quite simply. 'We want you to stay.'

As she watched Joyce leave the room, Vicky sighed. She was content with her life in Edinburgh, she really was. And she'd been so unhappy when she'd lived in Aberbrig before. It made sense that she wanted to go back.

Didn't it?

Doubts started nag at her.

She went to Paula's café for her lunch, just as she usually did.

'I've have the soup, please,' she said when Paula came over to take her order.

'Good choice. Heather's busy with Denny at the moment, so she hasn't been coming in. But Jack made this last night. He made some scones, too, if you fancy one.'

'Yes please,' Vicky agreed with a smile. 'Sounds like your husband-to-be is a handy man to have around.'

'Heather trained her boys well.' Paula grinned. 'They all worked here as teenagers, you know. Even Mark.'

Vicky had known — but even if she hadn't she might have guessed because she knew that Ryan was a terrific cook from the meals he'd made for her.

There she was, thinking about him again. He was barely out of her mind at any point, day or night. She even dreamt about him. Which made the waking hours, and the reality that they were no longer together, even harder to bear.

'I've been thinking about the wedding,' she said when Paula came back with her soup.

Paula's interest was evident as she moved her head to one side to hear what Vicky as about to say.

'What about the wedding?' she asked, a soft smile playing about her lips at the unexpected reminder of her big day.

'Well.' Vicky paused and cleared her throat, playing for time. 'It was so kind of you to invite me, but you asked me because of Ryan. And I don't think it's appropriate for me to go now.'

Paula set the order down then took a seat.

'We've all been wondering,' she said. 'And I hope you don't mind me asking. But what happened? You were so perfect for each other. And it's obvious Ryan's crazy about you. Though he refuses to talk about it.'

Vicky shook her head. This was too hard. She didn't want to discuss what had gone wrong.

'It was me,' she said at last. 'I was an idiot.'

Paula reached out and patted her hand.

'We're all idiots at times,' she said

227

kindly. 'Especially where men are concerned. But there's still time for you to make this right.'

Vicky wasn't sure.

'You can make a start at the wedding,' Paula added. 'Because the invitation was for you as yourself — and it still stands.'

How could she turn down an offer so kindly made?

'What's up?' Josh asked as she arrived back at the surgery.

She quickly told him about her misgivings over attending Paula's wedding.

'It's going to be a good day,' he told her. 'The whole of Kinbrae will be there.'

As will Ryan, she thought silently.

As she watched, Josh's expression cleared.

'Ah, I understand,' he said at last. 'Ryan McGregor.'

'Exactly.'

'Well, you don't have to worry, he won't cause a scene — he's not the type.'

'I know that. It's just, well, I don't

want to make things awkward for him. And seeing him there will be difficult. Especially as I'll be there on my own. What will I do if he brings someone?'

The thought had been on the fringes of her awareness since they'd decided not to see each other again. He'd have a perfect right to bring a 'plus one' and it would be none of her business. But the thought made her heart ache.

'I'll be there on my own,' Josh told her kindly. 'We can sit together. And maybe we can dance.'

'Thanks, Josh.' She smiled, feeling a little less alone. But she knew that even while Josh was a lovely man, he was no Ryan McGregor.

★　★　★

Vicky still knew it wasn't a good idea for her to attend the wedding, whatever Claire and Paula said. But Paula was the bride and she wanted Vicky there. And, of course, Vicky knew herself that she would be needed to keep an eye on

Steven during the times Claire was performing her bridesmaid duties.

Claire had gone off to get ready with the other bridesmaids — Paula's soon-to-be step-daughter, Jess, and a friend from down south — and she was to arrive in the car that had been arranged for the three of them. So, Vicky drove herself and Steven to the ceremony and helped him to a pew at the back of the tiny church.

'Are you alright?' she asked him as he sat down and winced.

'Just a twinge,' he dismissed.

But Vicky knew he had to still be in some pain — even if his condition was much improved and even if the doctors were very pleased and impressed with his recovery so far.

She took a deep breath and concentrated on trying to ignore Ryan. She could see the three red-haired brothers at the front: the back of Ryan's head was unmistakeable, even next to the other two.

And her heart ached.

She bravely turned towards her brother-in-law and smiled.

'The bride should be here soon,' she told Steven, in an attempt to divert her own attention.

And, on cue, the music heralded the arrival of the bridal party.

They all turned to look and, as one, everyone sighed. Paula was breathtakingly beautiful in a floor-length ivory lace gown. And, despite the chilly air outside, her bare arms showed no sign of goose bumps. Indeed, she was radiant. She walked into the church, a nervous smile visible behind her veil, on the arm of an older woman who, judging by how much she looked like Paula, had to be her mother.

The bridesmaids followed and Claire glanced across as she passed by and winked at Steven — who grinned in reply.

Again, Vicky wished she could find for herself a warm and secure relationship, such as her sister and brother-in-law shared.

With another deep breath, she made a concerted effort to keep her attention on proceedings. But, however hard she tried, her attention was drawn to Ryan.

He was one of Jack's best men — the other being the middle brother, Mark. All three McGregors stood tall and proud, in their kilts, each as handsome as the next. But Ryan, as far as Vicky was concerned, had the edge on all of them.

As she watched him, he turned, his gaze zeroing in on hers with military precision. It was almost as though he'd felt her eyes on him. But that was nonsense. Who could feel a glance? Or someone staring purposefully, even. Which, if she was honest, was exactly what she'd been doing.

She knew she should look away. But she didn't. And neither did he. Instead, the hint of a smile lifted the corners of his mouth. Without quite knowing how, she found herself smiling back.

There was no chance of Vicky paying

attention to the wedding vows after that.

★ ★ ★

'How are things, Steven?' Josh had approached Vicky and Steven as they stood by to watch Claire being photographed with the other bridesmaids and the two best men.

Steven grinned.

'Well, I couldn't have stood this long even last week,' he said. 'So I must be getting better.'

'You've made a remarkable recovery,' Josh smiled. 'Though don't overdo things today,' he cautioned. 'There's still some way to go before you're back to full fitness.'

'Yes, Doctor,' Steven said with a grin and Josh laughed.

'A GP's never off duty,' he said by way of an excuse for his concern. 'It's good to see Denny looking so well, too.'

Vicky followed his glance over to

where Denny stood with Heather and she nodded.

'I suspect he's still working too hard, despite medical advice,' Vicky confided, her brow creasing. She knew the haulage business had run into difficulties recently because Ryan had told her. Things had been so serious a little while ago that Heather had been forced to sell the café.

Not that it hadn't all worked out in the end — it was the sale of the café that had brought Paula into the McGregor's lives. And, looking at how happy the family members were at this wedding, there was no doubt in Vicky's mind that it had been a good thing.

'I'll have a word with Heather later,' Josh said.

While the photographs were still being taken, the three of them walked over to the village hall, which had been decorated with flowers and balloons ready for the reception.

Vicky appreciated Josh's company; she knew it wouldn't be good for

Steven to remain on his feet for long, but she also knew he would be reluctant to be the first to leave the churchyard. But, with the doctor walking with them, chatting as they went, the progression from church yard to the reception was a natural one.

Paula had made sure Vicky was seated between Steven and Josh and she gave silent thanks to her friend for being so thoughtful when she must have had so much else on her mind. Vicky knew she wouldn't be short of conversation, sitting between the two — and she hoped that would mean she wouldn't be constantly looking for a glimpse of Ryan.

That hope was cruelly dashed when the others started to arrive.

Her breath caught as she saw him come into the hall and she couldn't take her eyes from him. He was so tall, so handsome — all the other men paled by comparison. He was with Faye, the two of them laughing and joking.

He didn't even glance her way. And her heart cracked a little more.

* * *

Wherever Ryan looked, his glance seemed to return to Vicky. She sat between Steven and Josh and she exchanged the occasional word with them as they watched the bridal couple take to the floor for their first dance.

He couldn't look away. He hated that — she'd finished their relationship, told him she didn't want to be with him. Yet he was still pining after her like some lovesick puppy.

He made a conscious effort to smile and forced himself to look about the place. With Jack and Paula's first dance finished, other couples were moving onto the floor.

As he was trying to ignore the urge to go and ask Vicky to dance, a hand reached out and took his.

'Come and dance with me,' Faye said as she pulled him to his feet.

He smiled into his friend's face.

'Why not,' he shrugged, and allowed her to lead him to the dance floor. If the girl he loved didn't want to dance with him, he didn't really want to dance at all. But he couldn't be seen to mope at his own brother's wedding.

For today he had to put a brave face on his misery. There would be plenty of time to wallow in the days and months to come. And, once Vicky had left the area, living without her would be even more unbearable.

At least, for the moment, he was able to catch a glimpse of her occasionally.

By some huge misfortune Faye chose to take the path that would lead them directly past where Vicky sat. He slowed as he drew level with her table and their eyes met. At that point, Faye let go of his hand.

'How are you?' he asked her. Up close she looked tired — he could see faint purple markings under her eyes that hinted at sleepless nights.

She smiled up at him and something

passed between them that let him hope. She still had feelings for him. He knew it. Nobody could look at another person the way she was looking at him and not mean it.

'I'm good,' she said. 'How are you?'

'Yes, fine.' It was ridiculous — he was reduced to general chit-chat with the woman who meant most to him in the world.

He felt Faye's supportive hand on his arm and he turned his head to find the other woman looking inquisitively at him — as though she couldn't quite understand what was happening between him and Vicky.

'You promised me a dance,' she said.

He quickly glanced back at Vicky and her frosty stare wasn't lost on him.

'Don't let me keep you,' she said.

But he was reluctant to leave her.

'Maybe we could dance later?' he suggested.

'Perhaps,' she agreed.

And the fact her reply hadn't been an outright 'no' gave him even more hope.

'What are you doing?' Faye hissed into his ear once they were a safe distance away.

He shook his head. He'd never seen her so cross.

'What do you mean?'

'Vicky's made it perfectly clear she wants nothing to do with you.'

He didn't need reminding about that.

'We're still friends,' he said. 'Besides, why are you so concerned?'

Faye sighed and they began to dance.

'If she doesn't want you, there are plenty of people who do.'

He stopped dead, mid-step.

'What on earth are you talking about?'

Faye leaned towards him to speak to him — he guessed because the music was loud.

'Some of us think you're pretty hot,' she said. And he could see her face flush, even in the low light of the dance floor.

'Faye,' he told her gently. 'We're friends, you and I. Nothing more.' He loved Faye to pieces, but it was purely platonic on his side. He'd never even suspected in all the time he'd known her that she had deeper feelings.

'But it could be more . . .'

'No.' He was adamant. 'If anything was going to happen between the two of us then it would have done years ago. When we first met.'

'You weren't interested in a relationship back then. Besides, you could learn to have feelings for me. You didn't love Vicky when you first met.'

'That's different.' He struggled for a moment to find the right words. Life would be so simple if he could feel that way about Faye. But, instead, he was completely smitten with a woman who didn't love him enough to stay.

Faye stepped away from him — as far away as she could with all the dancing couples around them.

'I've made a bit of an idiot of myself, haven't I?'

'No,' he insisted. 'Of course you haven't.' He reached out and took her hand, pulling her towards him and leading the way in a waltz — which must have looked a bit out of place considering the song had a disco beat.

Faye threw her head back and laughed, before enthusiastically dancing along.

'See? You behave like this and then you expect women not to love you.'

'You can love me all you like,' he said with a grin. 'In the same way I love you — as a friend.'

'OK, Ryan McGregor,' she said. 'But if you ever change your mind . . . '

He knew he wouldn't. There was no way he could feel about Faye the way he felt about Vicky. But it would be cruel to rub that in when he'd already told her there was no chance for the two of them.

'I'll bear it in mind,' he told her and winked at her. He knew they'd be fine — that their friendly relationship hadn't been ruined by Faye's confession — when she laughed.

As they circled the floor, he couldn't

resist glancing over to see if Vicky was watching.

She was.

* * *

It shouldn't upset her so much to see Ryan having fun with another woman, but it did. She'd met Faye a number of times — and she'd liked her. And, all those times, she hadn't even thought that the other woman had been attracted to Ryan.

Tonight, though, she got the feeling that their relationship had shifted. Faye seemed more than friendly — and Ryan didn't seem to be fighting her off. And the ease with which they had interacted in the past seemed to have been replaced by something else. Something that had Faye smiling softly at Ryan.

This didn't make Vicky happy.

'What do you think, Vicky?' Steven saying her name forced her attention to the two men she was seated beside, but she didn't have a clue what she was supposed to offer an opinion about.

'I'm sorry, I was miles away.'

'We were just saying it's a lovely wedding,' Josh filled in gently. 'So nice for the villagers to have the opportunity to party.'

She forced herself to keep her eyes averted from Ryan. Whatever he was up to, it was none of her business now.

'It's quite the nicest wedding I've ever been to,' she replied, not untruthfully. The McGregors had made everyone so welcome. And it was no secret that Vicky thought very highly of the bride: Paula had been one of the people who had helped to make her temporary move back to the area bearable and she always looked forward to lunchtimes when she could pop into the café.

Josh sat back and looked at her thoughtfully.

'Now that you've seen what a terrific village Kinbrae is, have you — by any chance — reconsidered your decision to leave us once Steven's fit and well?'

Vicky hadn't been expecting that. She'd thought she'd made her position clear. Her mouth settled into a silent 'oh' and she stared helplessly at Josh. He laughed good-naturedly.

'That will be a 'no', then. Well, you can't blame a guy for trying,' he said. 'You've settled in very well, it would be a shame if you left us so soon. Even Joyce Imrie's taken to you — and she's a very difficult customer to please.'

Vicky smiled.

'I like Joyce,' she admitted. 'Underneath all the bluster she's a sweetheart.'

'Just think about what I said,' Josh pleaded. 'The offer of a permanent job's there and there's no need to make a decision straight away.'

14

Last Dance

Vicky became aware of someone standing over her. She knew who it would be before she even turned her head. And, when she did look up, her breath caught: he was breathtakingly gorgeous. The impact close up was almost more than she could take.

'Dance with me?' he said as he held out his hand to her.

She reached out and their fingers met, but she didn't move from her seat.

'I told Claire I'd stay with Steven until she got back. She's gone to help Paula get changed into her going away outfit.' Still her fingers clung to his — she simply couldn't stop herself.

'I'm fine,' Steven told her. 'You go and dance.'

'And I'm here if Steven does need

anything,' Josh added helpfully.

It seemed everyone thought she should dance with Ryan.

Besides, Steven was right — he was fine. He'd probably been fine for quite a while, but she'd been too busy to notice. OK, his full rehabilitation would take some time, but he was certainly well enough that Claire would cope if Vicky went back to her own life.

The realisation was crushing — because leaving Aberbrig meant she'd never run into Ryan again.

Slowly she got to her feet.

What harm would one dance do? There was no way, after all, she could hurt any more than she was already.

'OK,' she said and she watched in utter fascination as his lips curved upwards. And that was when she realised exactly the harm that one dance could do — because she knew then, once Ryan took her in his arms, she'd never want him to let her go.

'Won't Faye mind you dancing with

me?' she asked and squirmed as Ryan raised an eyebrow. Had the question been too revealing of the fact she'd been watching the two of them getting cosy? 'I mean,' she rushed to explain, her face warming, 'you did bring her, didn't you?'

He grinned.

'Yes, in the same way you brought Josh. And he doesn't seem to mind the two of us dancing together.'

'It looked like there was more to you and Faye than friendship a few minutes ago.' And she could have bitten off her tongue — she'd incriminated herself. Shown herself up for what she was — a jealous ex-girlfriend.

But Ryan didn't gloat. He looked straight into her eyes — and her heart hammered in her chest.

'Faye's not your rival. She knows we'll only ever be friends.'

With that assurance, she let him lead her onto the floor. Relief was over-whelming and she hadn't known until then just how much she'd feared she'd lost him to the other woman.

He put his hands on her waist and she leaned in close and lifted her own around his neck. It felt good. She sighed against him.

'How have you been?' he asked as they danced.

'Fine,' she replied, but she knew her voice held no conviction. 'How about you?'

'Not brilliant,' he admitted and she wished she hadn't returned the question. She didn't want to know that she'd hurt him.

'I'm sorry,' she said as she bit into her lip.

'I know,' he said.

He looked down at her and she couldn't believe she'd been so stupid as to tell him she didn't want to be with him. That she'd thought being without him would be a better option than moving to live permanently in Aberbrig. Because the truth was there was nothing on earth that could be worse than being without Ryan McGregor.

It was only a pity it had taken her so long to realise that.

Then he sighed and gathered her close.

And she let him.

* * *

They were all tired when they arrived back at the house — particularly Steven. And he was in considerable pain after the exertions of the day so he went to bed as soon as they got home.

Claire saw him settled, then stayed up to talk over the day with Vicky over a cup of tea in the living room.

'You know,' she began, sinking back into the sofa, 'it's daft.'

'What's daft?' Vicky kicked off her shoes and rubbed her aching feet.

'You and Ryan. It's clear for anyone to see that you're both crazy about each other. I don't understand why you don't stop all the nonsense and just get together.'

Vicky was surprised to hear her sister

speak so bluntly.

'I'm only here until Steven gets better,' she reminded Claire weakly, neatly ignoring the fact she'd now realised she was no longer needed here.

'That's a rubbish excuse,' Claire said. 'Finding someone special is so hard — someone you love and who loves you back. And it's especially hard to find someone who's nice and will treat you right. It's not true what they say about fish in the sea, you know ... You're very lucky to have met Ryan. It's criminal to let him go so easily.'

'And what do we do when I move back to Edinburgh'?

Claire shook her head.

'You make it work — that's what you do. Either long-distance, or maybe you even decide Aberbrig's not as bad as you remember and you decide to stay.'

Vicky had guessed this suggestion would be on Claire's agenda again at some point. And she'd thought she would argue the point. As she had whenever anyone had made the suggestion up until now.

But, what really did she have to go back for?

She had friends, but she could keep in touch with them quite easily.

What was left of her family was here. She'd made friends in the area. She had the offer to make her job permanent — a job she loved. But the clincher was that Ryan was here.

She didn't want to leave him. She loved him. And she wanted to be with him — even if that meant moving back to Aberbrig.

She got to her feet.

'I have to speak to Ryan.'

Claire's eyes widened.

'What, now? It's gone one in the morning.'

'I don't care. I need to speak to him now — before I change my mind.'

Claire opened her mouth and Vicky guessed she was going to ask what Vicky might change her mind about. But, before she could speak, the buzzing of Vicky's mobile interrupted her.

Vicky snatched up her bag and dug the phone out.

Her breath caught as she saw the name on the display: Ryan.

'Did I wake you?' he asked when she answered.

'No, Claire and I were talking.'

'I'm outside. I need to talk to you. Can I come in?'

'Yes, I'll meet you at the front door in two seconds.' She turned to her sister. 'Ryan's outside — he wants to talk.'

Claire grinned then shook her head. 'Well go let him in.'

By the time Vicky returned to the living room with Ryan in her wake, Claire had made herself scarce.

'She must have gone to bed,' Vicky told him, hating that she was making small talk at a time when she needed to have the most important conversation of her life.

'Good, because I need to speak to you alone.' He took her hands in both of his and his eyes met hers. 'If I thought . . . ' He stopped speaking for a moment then sighed and carried on. 'If I thought for one minute that letting you go would make you happy, then I wouldn't be saying this. But I think you feel as I do — that you want to be with me as much as I want to be with you.'

Vicky's heart was beating wildly and she tried to speak, but her words choked her and refused to form on her tongue. In the end she nodded.

His lips twitched into the hint of a smile and Vicky felt herself smiling back at him.

'I don't care where we live,' he said. 'If you don't want to live around here, then that's fine. I understand you weren't happy here as a teenager; we can live wherever you want.'

Happiness threatened to overflow. She could barely believe what she was hearing.

'You'd leave your family? The job you love? To move away to be with me?'

He lifted her hands to his lips and kissed her fingers.

'I'd move to the end of the world to be with you.'

She shook her head — unable to take in what he was telling her.

His smile slipped.

'Is that a 'no'?'

'No — it's a 'yes'!' she cried as she snatched her hands back and threw them around his neck. 'Though I don't think we should move away from here. I don't think your family would forgive me if I took you away.'

'They'd get over it.'

'But my family's here, too. When you called I was in the middle of telling Claire that I needed to speak to you — to tell you that I wanted to stay here, with you.'

His arms tightened around her.

'You hate this place,' he reminded her.

She sighed. She'd thought that was true for a long time and it had taken nearly letting the love of her life go to show her that it wasn't the case.

'Yes, Aberbrig has some very unhappy memories for me, but since I've been back I've been happy here. It's taken me until now to realise that.'

'So we can get married and live in Aberbrig? And you'll be OK with that?'

'Yes,' she squealed.

From somewhere near the door, she was aware of Claire shouting to Steven.

'She's said 'yes'. And they're not moving away.'

But Vicky was too busy kissing and being kissed by Ryan to take much notice.

THE END

We do hope that you have enjoyed reading this large print book.

Did you know that all of our titles are available for purchase?

We publish a wide range of high quality large print books including:
Romances, Mysteries, Classics
General Fiction
Non Fiction and Westerns

Special interest titles available in large print are:
The Little Oxford Dictionary
Music Book, Song Book
Hymn Book, Service Book

Also available from us courtesy of Oxford University Press:
Young Readers' Dictionary
(large print edition)
Young Readers' Thesaurus
(large print edition)

For further information or a free brochure, please contact us at:
Ulverscroft Large Print Books Ltd.,
The Green, Bradgate Road, Anstey,
Leicester, LE7 7FU, England.
Tel: (00 44) 0116 236 4325
Fax: (00 44) 0116 234 0205

Other titles in the
Linford Romance Library:

MISTRESS OF MELLIN COVE

Rena George

When Dewi Luscombe is rescued from a shipwreck by the young Master of Mellin Hall, Kit St Neot, she finds she has lost her memory and doesn't know who she is. Touched by the girl's vulnerability and confusion, Kit decides to help her. But Dewi is haunted by the thought that someone close to her died in the shipwreck, and she sets off with Kit to ride across Cornwall to discover her true identity. Will Dewi ever regain her memory? And will Kit return her growing feelings for him?

SWEET VENGEANCE

Roberta Grieve

Aspiring actress Kelley Robinson mistakes infatuation for love when she falls for charismatic media celebrity Carl Roche. Despite the warnings of her friends, she believes his promises and moves in with him. But when she discovers how he has deceived her, she is determined to get her revenge. Paul, a seemingly sympathetic journalist, offers to help put her plan into action. But is he only looking for a good story for his newspaper? Who can Kelley really trust?